BOWMAN'S KID

Lee Kershaw had a tough assignment. Bowman's kid would be hard to find. He might be anywhere from the Rockies to the Missouri—from the Canadian border to the Rio Grande. Lee Kershaw was a clever man— and a tough one. If anyone could find Bowman's kid he could. But was one man a match for the bloodthirsty gang who wanted Bowman's ranch bad enough to kill for it?

GORDON D. SHIRREFFS

BOWMAN'S KID

Complete and Unabridged

LINFORD
Leicester

First published in the U.S.A. in 1973 by
Fawcett Publications, Inc.

First Linford Edition
published January 1987
by arrangement with
Ballantine Books,
A Division of Random House, Inc,
New York.

British Library CIP Data

Shirreffs, Gordon D.
    Bowman's kid.—Large print ed.—(Linford
western library)
    I. Title
    813'.54[F]   PS3569.H562

    ISBN 0-7089-6343-9

Published by
F. A. Thorpe (Publishing) Ltd.
Anstey, Leicestershire
Set by Rowland Phototypesetting Ltd.
Bury St. Edmunds, Suffolk
Printed and bound in Great Britain by
T. J. Press (Padstow) Ltd., Padstow, Cornwall

1

SOMEONE or something was being stalked in the darkness of the New Mexican night. There was an uneasy, unnameable feeling in the graveyard quiet. Lee Kershaw ground-reined the tired dun. A ridge of broken rock sawtoothed its low crest against the night sky. Lee replaced his boots with his *n-deh b'keh*, the thigh-length, thick-soled, button-toed desert footgear of the Apache. He folded down the thigh parts and tied them in place just below his knees. Nothing moved except the distant, flickering light of the ice-ship stars against the dark sky.

It was Mescalero country, and the Mescaleros were rumoured to be restless and making war talk in their mountain eyrie just to the north; but they would not hunt for man or game at night. The most favorable time to hunt the white man was when the first pewter-hued traces of the false dawn tinted the eastern sky. That was the time when the white man's energy and spirits were at their lowest ebb, and the

White-Eye was soft for the killing. And if by chance it was the Mescalero who was killed at dawn light, his soul would not be doomed to wander in the Shadow Land during eternity.

The dun nudged Lee with his nose. The two big, blanket-covered canteens were empty—*dry* empty. The waterhole was over the ridge and deep hidden by the darkness. Lee withdrew his Winchester '73 from the saddle scabbard and levered a round of .44/40 into the chamber. He let the hammer down to half cock.

Lee had come north from Fort Davis in Texas, riding and walking at night to avoid the heat of the late summer and the threat of the predatory Lipans, who were raiding into West Texas. Lee had come north because a man had come to him in a Fort Davis saloon and asked him to meet a *vaquero*, one Vicente Galeras, at Tinaja del Muerto on the second Wednesday of the month. Now, whether or not he met Vicente Galeras at the *tinaja* over the ridge did not really matter, at least for the moment. It was the water that mattered, as it always did in that dry and broken land.

Lee catfooted up the slope with the warm and fitful night wind blowing against him. He shoved back his hat and let it hang between his shoulders by the chin strap. He went to ground just below the crest, then inched forward, using a ragged bunching of gramma grass on the crest for cover.

The *tinaja* was in a dark and haunted hollow at the base of a limestone rock formation that somehow managed to seep good clear water into the shallow rock pans, or *tinajas*, at the foot of the formation. It was not a good place. The water had saved lives, but it had also cost lives. The early Spanish explorers had learned that fact the hard way. The Mescaleros had used the spring for centuries as a death trap for both men and animals. The Spaniards, with their macabre skill in geographical nomenclature, had named the haunted place Tinaja del Muerto—the Jar of Death. The place had never failed to live up to its name and evil reputation.

Something down at the spring rustled drily, like a cricket testing its reedy night song.

The man had found Lee drinking alone in the Fort Davis saloon. Lee had just finished a dirty and dangerous job along the Rio Grande, and his springs needed unwinding with the lubrication of much fiery brandy. "Duke Bowman needs you at the Broken Bow, Kershaw," the stranger had said. "But don't go

3

straight there. A man by the name of Vicente Galeras, a *vaquero* of the Broken Bow, will meet you at Tinaja del Muerto on the second Wednesday of this month." He had placed a curious silver button in Lee's hand. "This button will identify you."

Lee had looked down at the button. "Who says I am going at all?"

"Only this," the man had replied, covering the silver button with ten crisp one hundred dollar bills. "I was told this is your usual first week's fee."

Lee watched with faint amusement. "And who are you?"

"My name does not matter. I am a lawyer who has done some services for Duke Bowman. I received the money and the button by registered mail in El Paso. I had already planned to move my practice to Forth Worth. It is just as well. If I returned to El Paso, I might be signing my own death warrant. They may not know for sure I contacted you for Duke Bowman, but I'm not taking any chances."

"Who are *they*?"

The legal eagle had looked quickly right and left, and then behind himself, and had lowered his voice. "The Dakins," he had said.

"There's something loco about this. The Dakins, brothers, cousins, and other shirttail kin, have been the heart of Bowman's Running MB *corrida* for at least twenty years."

"Times have changed. The old *corrida* is gone, at least the native New Mexicans are, leaving the Dakins, and they are trying to take over the Broken Bow."

Lee had carefully placed the silver button on the table and had covered it with the bills. "Take back his money and his goddamned trick silver button, mister. I'd rather work for the Devil himself than for Duke Bowman."

The stranger had nodded. "Bowman mentioned the possibility of this in his letter. But he also wrote: 'Let the money talk to Lee Kershaw. That's his kind of language.'" The stranger had stood up and emptied his glass. "If you do go, Kershaw, *watch your back*." When Lee had looked up from the tempting pile of money, the only indication that the stranger had been there was the batwing door still swinging from his hasty exit.

That same night Lee Kershaw had ridden north with a cool thousand dollars and a peculiar silver button in his shirt pocket. Perhaps it was more for curiosity's sake than

5

for money that he headed out to Tinaja del Muerto—curiosity to meet a *vaquero* whom he had vaguely known long ago and to learn why Duke Bowman, the *muy hombre* of the Broken Bow, needed Lee Kershaw, manhunter.

A man coughed softly in the darkness near the *tinaja*.

The dried gramma grass on the ridge crest moved a little, and its shadow lightened.

Lee bellied on loose blow sand between boulders still warm from the heat of the day's sun, hoping to God he would not run into a night-hunting sidewinder, which bites quickly without the honest, strident warning of rattles.

The scent of a man came to Lee, compounded of stale sweat, tobacco smoke, dusty leather, and just a hint of fermented horseshit for piquancy—*Parfum de Vaquero*. He moved forward in silence.

The rifle muzzle touched the nape of the *vaquero*'s neck. "Do not move," Lee's soft voice warned. "Open your left hand." A silver button was placed in the palm.

"*Gracias a Dios*," whispered the *vaquero*. "Señor Kershaw?"

"You have the button," replied Lee.

6

The wind sprang up quickly. The sere brush across the *tinaja* rustled drily like the mating song of crickets.

"Don't move suddenly," warned Lee.

A rifle muzzle across the *tinaja* flamed, and the crack of the explosion mingled with what seemed to be the sound of a stick being suddenly whipped into thick mud. The *vaquero* turned left and flung up his right arm. He was hard hit and made no sound when he went down. The shot's echo died away, and the smell of burnt powder drifted on the wind.

Lee felt the warm and sticky wetness on the man's chest. "What does Duke Bowman want of me?" whispered Lee.

His answer was a thick and liquid cough that sprayed his face with a warm froth. "Talk, damn you!" urged Lee. The man moved a little. "I was to guide you in to see him secretly." Lee bent close. "But why?" he asked. "They mustn't know why he sent for you," gasped Galeras. The *vaquero*'s head dropped forever.

Lee pried open the clenched hand of the dead man and removed the button from it. There was the faintest of scraping sounds on the blow sand, and then it was deathly quiet again—the usual brooding quietness of Tinaja del Muerto.

A man had died there that dark night. *Bueno*! The spring was sated—for a time.

The dun raised his head and slanted forward his ears. A lean shadow drifted noiselessly through the darkness. Lee unhooked the canteens from the saddle. Something moved on the ridge crest. Lee faded behind a boulder. Leather scraped against rock on the ridge. Lee reached out and rifle slapped the dun across his rump. The dun obediently trotted toward the west and away from the ridge.

A rifle exploded flame and smoke on the ridge. The shot echo slammed back and forth between the canyons walls. The dun galloped off into the darkness.

"Keep on going, Kershaw!" yelled a hoarse voice. "Don't come back, *manhunter*! Hawww! Hawww! Hawww!"

The boulder stood alone in the darkness.

The sound of the dun's hoofs rataplaning on the hard ground died away in the darkness to the west.

The sound of voices came from the *tinaja*. Water splashed.

"Let Galeras lie there for the buzzards and the coyotes," said a hoarse-voiced man. "Serves

8

him right for thinkin' he could fool me, Chisos."

"He shoulda known better than that, Cass," a dry Texas voice said.

"If that really was Lee Kershaw," put in another voice, tinged with the soft archaic Spanish accent of a native New Mexican, "he will come back."

"I scared the hell outa him," blustered Cass Dakin. "He won't come back, Nuno."

"Maybe," said Nuno doubtfully. "Would it not be better to make sure of him? Two dead men, in this case, are far better than one."

"He won't be back," insisted Cass. Hoofs rattled like pebbles in a gourd. In a little while, the sound of the hoofs died away to the east.

The *tinaja* sank back into its habitual brooding quietness.

2

THE faint sound of bubbling, slobbering water came from the darkened Tinaja del Muerto and then died away.

Lee stoppered his canteens and dragged the body of Vicente Galeras back from the *tinaja* into a deep cleft in the rocks. He risked lighting a candle. He frisked the stiffening body and set aside a pint flask and a pack of Lobo Negro cigarettes. He snapped the dirty string that held a green-hued, imitation silver cross about the *vaquero*'s neck. He had recognized Galeras as one of the best of the Broken Bow *corrida*, or the worst, depending on whether you were a friend or an enemy of Duke Bowman. He had been one of the loyal ones, a man whose god was Duke Bowman. The imitation silver cross had likely been only lip service to that other god.

Lee took a flat velvet-covered case from the *vaquero*'s shirt pocket. He opened it to look at a beautiful, dark-haired young woman of perhaps eighteen years of age and a sober, big-eyed boy

10

of perhaps three or four years of age standing beside her, brave in velvet trousers, high black stockings, and button shoes. He wore a neat little *charro*-type jacket with six large silver buttons. As closely as Lee could tell, the buttons were exactly the same as the one he had in his shirt pocket.

The dun whinnied softly through the darkness.

Lee dragged the body deeper into the cleft and covered it with loose rock. He watered the dun and then led him through the limestone formation to a spot where the mountains to the east could be seen. He fed the dun and then threw a blanket on the ground. He fell asleep with his half-cocked Winchester on one side of him and his Colt in his left hand.

Lee awoke when the wind shifted. There was a faint grayish cast in the eastern sky beyond the looming mountains. He ate a little and then shaped and lit a cigarette. The dawn grew swiftly across the arid land as he smoked.

Thirty miles to the west of Tinaja del Muerto there were mountains, and beyond them the Rio Grande, the only water in all that distance.

Faint dust wreathed up close to the base of the notched pass in the eastern mountains. That pass led over the mountains to the Broken Bow country. There were two alternatives known to Lee by which he might reach that country without risking the pass. He could go south and round the end of the mountains on the Texas side of the Texas-New Mexico Territory border. He could go north for twenty miles through the dry and waterless country to a shallow pass that cut through the northern end of the range. On the far side of that pass, perhaps fifteen miles to the south, was Ribbon Creek; but there might not be water there, for it was a time of great drought.

The sun warmed the empty land. The limestone mountain range rose six thousand feet above the desert country, the upper two thousand feet forming an almost sheer escarpment. On the eastern side was the great *estancia* of Duke Bowman, the Running MB, better know as the Broken Bow, from the river which gave the range its name. It was the best ranch country on that side of the mountains. It was perpetually watered, heavily timbered, and rich with mineral deposits. The man Mark Bowman, better known as Duke, had seized that rich land thirty-five years past from the Mescaleros, whose natural heritage it had been. He had driven Indi-yi-yahn, the almost legendary Mescalero war chief, from that valley and in later years had killed him with his own hands.

Lee took out the silver button and studied it in the growing light. The embossed design was intricate and curious—a pair of script letters M & B, or in rangeland parlance, a Running MB. The letters passed through a stylized bow, broken in the arc by the interposing letters.

"What would Duke Bowman want of me?" mused Lee.

He looked again at the eastern mountains between him and the Broken Bow. They stretched north and south for seventy-five miles with the highest and most rugged part just over the Texas line dramatically culminating in a towering eight thousand-foot peak. The mass of the range, however, was in New Mexico Territory, extending northward in the shape of a gigantic ridge that was gashed with twisted canyons, sheer plunging slopes and drops, and towering cliff faces. The view from the west could easily deceive one into thinking that the eastern face was the same barren wilderness of limestone rock, but on the eastern side, the slopes gentled into deep, pine-forested canyons and clear, running streams.

"Go home," the mind voice warned.

Lee lit another cigarette.

"Duke Bowman breaks all men," added the voice. "*All* men . . ."

No one but a fool, or a madman, *or* Lee Kershaw would attempt a crossing of the burning, arid country to the north to reach the north pass of the range.

"There are the Dakins," warned the voice.

Marsh Dakin was a hard, dour man, Texas bred, who had ramrodded the notorious Broken Bow *corrida* for over twenty years, backed by his younger half-brothers Sid and Cass, and his much younger cousins, Ben and Charles, the latter nicknamed Reata. There were others— shirttail kin, Pecos River men. They had all the vices of a highland clan and none of the virtues, except loyalty to Duke Bowman, and that now seemed to be gone.

Lee led the dun down the slope to a long, low ridge which would shield him from anyone looking west from the mountains.

By noon, the baking, rocky soil seemed to be lifting and wavering in the heat-shimmering atmosphere like a flapping blanket. The thin dust rose about man and horse. The sun reflected up from the ground to burn into Lee's eyes and into his very brain, seeking to strike him down.

3

CASS DAKIN lowered his battered field glasses and looked back over his shoulder. "That's a dust devil," he said.

"How can you be sure?" asked Nuno Mercado. "The dust is always behind that ridge, and it keeps moving north."

A lean young man squatted teetering on his bootheels, rolling a quirly. His light blue eyes, seemingly as guileless as those of a baby, looked down the long, heat-shimmering pass toward the illusive thread of dust drifting upward on the lower ground. "The wind is blowing from the northwest," he said.

"I still say it's a dust devil, Chisos," insisted Cass.

Nuno Mercado eased his sweating crotch. "Mother of the Devil," he cursed. "This place is the hallway to hell!"

"Imagine how it is out there," said Chisos as he lit up.

"I run Kershaw off last night," said Cass.

"That so?" asked Chisos politely. "Then how

16

come we ain't seen no dust devils to the west or the southwest?"

Cass eyed the young Texan. "I say he turned back."

Chisos didn't play the game. "Just as you say, Cass." He stood up. "But if that dust out there *is* Kershaw, and he gets around these mountains to reach the Broken Bow, you'll have a helluva time explainin' it to Marsh, and what's worse, your sister Stella. Personally, I'd rather explain it to him than to her."

"They ain't tellin' me what to do!"

Chisos yawned a little and covered his mouth with his hand. "That so?" he softly asked.

No one but a fool, or a madman, *or* Lee Kershaw would cross that devil's furnace in the heat of the late summer at a time of great drought. The thought was that of Nuno Mercado. "There is no water down there," he said, almost as though to reassure himself that Lee Kershaw would not attempt the crossing.

Cass turned away from the cool and level stare of Chisos, glad of some excuse to break the contact. "See?" he said triumphantly. "He can't get to water for two days, and he can't live out there without water for even one day."

"Unless he tries for North Pass," put in Chisos.

"No," insisted Cass. "I outsmarted him. I figured he was headin' for Tinaja del Muerto, and I was right."

"Anyone could have figured that," argued Chisos. "*And*, he's still alive."

"But Galeras ain't! Whatever the old man told Galeras to tell Kershaw, he never had a chance to tell him, did he?"

"We can't be sure of that," said Nuno. "There *is* someone down there, moving to the northeast," he added firmly.

"It's Kershaw then," said Chisos with conviction. "He knows the old man wants to see him, and by Jesus, he's goin' to see him!"

"I still say he's gone west!" shouted Cass, all mouth and no reason.

Chisos mounted his horse. "Well, you're the *patrón*," he said.

"Where the hell do you think you're goin'?" snapped Cass.

"Back to the Broken Bow."

"I ain't said we should!"

"Well, in that case, just what the hell do you aim to gain by sittin' around here fryin' your ass?"

18

"Kershaw still might try to get through this pass."

"God give me strength," murmured Chisos.

"Well, what would you do?" demanded Cass.

"I thought you'd never ask! Kershaw is either holed up down at Tinaja del Muerto waitin' for darkness, or that's him raisin' that dust down there. I think that's him, headin' for North Pass. He's tryin' for Ribbon Creek. We'd better get back to the Broken Bow and have Marsh send some of the boys up that way to get him there. If Kershaw lives through today, you can bet your ass he'll head for Ribbon Creek."

Chisos was right, but Cass Dakin fancied himself a leader of hard men—like Duke Bowman had once been and like his older brothers, Marsh and Sid, were now, to say nothing of his older sister Stella. He was jealous of Chisos Martin. The young Texan had just turned twenty-one in the past month. Five years younger than Cass, he was already showing signs of leadership and had caught Marsh's eye more than once, to Cass's embarrassment. "Ain't no living man can get across that desert this time of year," he said.

"Want to bet ten bucks?" asked Chisos.

"Don't bet," said Nuno to Cass. "This man

19

Kershaw is not human. He can do things no living man can do. Some of my people claim he is a *brujo*—a male witch. They say he can turn himself into anything he likes. It is also said, on good authority, by a priest I happen to know, that he can make himself invisible . . . ."

Chisos doubled up with laughter as he handed a ten to Nuno. "Put up or shut up, Cass," he invited.

Cass handed the ten to Nuno. "One of these days," he murmured.

Chisos eyed the big man. "How fast is Kershaw with the sixgun, Nuno?" he asked over his shoulder. "As fast as me?"

"He is still alive in the most dangerous business in the world, that of hunting dangerous and desperate men."

"You didn't answer my question."

Cass looked at the cocky young Texan. "There's always someone, somewhere, that's faster than fast guns like you, Chisos."

Chisos smiled. "I haven't met him yet."

"You will. You will," promised Cass.

Chisos laughed confidently as he rode up the pass. He had the supreme confidence of a man of twenty-one, from Texas; he had neatly filed five notches on the butt of his Colt in the past three years, and Chisos, with true Texas arrogance, *never* counted cholos or Indians.

4

THE massive limestone house overlooked the Broken Bow where the river rushed in a great arc from the narrow canyon thrust into the looming mountain behind the ranch. The almost perfect arc of the river had long ago been broken by a gigantic collapse of the limestone cliffs that beetled across the river from the level ground where the ranch buildings were located. The rock fall had formed a natural dam, which had in time been circumvented by the river, thus giving the river, the valley, and, in time, the Running MB Ranch the name of Broken Bow.

The great limestone *casa* was ramparted like a medieval fortress, and on diagonally opposite corners of the flat roof, Duke Bowman had built sqaut towers, each of which provided covering fire along two sides of the house. Loopholes pierced the house and tower walls, and the few windows were fitted with heavy shutters.

Beyond the *casa* was a dark *bosque* of cotton-woods and willows, and on the fringe of the *bosque* were the older log buildings of the ranch. Only two lights shone through the darkness—one in the original low *casa*, and the other in the northeast tower of the great limestone house.

The valley had long ago been the hereditary home of the Mescaleros. Thirty-five years earlier, before the Civil War, Mark Bowman had driven the Mescaleros from their home. Twenty years later, the Mescaleros, led by their great warrior chief Indi-yi-yahn—Killer of Enemies, had made the fatal mistake of trying to take back their ancestral home. Twenty-two blood stiffened scalps of thick, black, Mescalero hair had been hung on the barbed wire of the approaches to the Broken Bow. The legendary medicine shirt of the Mescaleros, worn that bloody day by Indi-yi-yahn to assure victory, had been stripped from his dead body by Duke Bowman, the man who had killed him in hand-to-hand combat, and hung on the wall of the tower room. The Mescaleros, in time, had put the twenty-two scalps in the backs of their memories; they had never forgotten the medicine shirt. Without it, the war power of the Mescaleros had been broken, and their good medicine gone forever.

Lee catfooted through the *bosque*. There was a haunting loneliness about the darkened *casa*. Faint light showed in the chinks of the northeast tower's shuttered windows, and a faint wraith of smoke drifted from its chimney.

Something moved in the shadows of the *bosque*.

Lee stopped.

The great dog growled deeply in his throat and charged.

Lee swung his Wincester barrel hard across the gaping fanged jaws of the beast. The dog raised its head upward and sideways. The razor-edged *cuchillo* sank into the left side of the dog's muscle-distended throat and ripped cleanly and easily across it. Lee leaped backward to avoid the spouting gush of dark blood. The dog fell heavily, thrashing powerfully with its hind legs among the thick layer of leaves. The butt of the Winchester dropped with killing force at the base of the dog's neck.

Lee stepped back. Nothing moved except the wind-disturbed leaves.

Lee dragged the heavy body to the river and dumped it in. It swirled out into the fast current in an easy curve toward the deep, dark waters that curled whitely at the base of the sheer limestone cliffs across the river. It sank at last, leaving a swirl of ghostly foam on the dark surface of the river.

stone cliffs across the river. It sank at last, leaving a swirl of ghostly foam on the dark surface of the river.

5

DUKE BOWMAN sat in a heavy, rawhide-covered chair, staring into the flickering, shifting kaleidoscope of color hovering over the thick bed of embers in the beehive fireplace. His big, liver-spotted hands rested almost lifelessly on the hardwood arms of the chair. An Argand lamp, turned low, stood on a table beside the chair. The light from the top of the lampshade shone on what seemed to be the headless and legless trunk of a gaunt body that hung on the wall above the fireplace, its outstretched arms in the shape of crucifixion. It was the dusty, bloodstained medicine shirt of Indi-yi-yahn, made from the well-tanned skins of two strangled fawns and decorated with the mystic symbols of sun, moon, rain, stars, water beetle, and spider, as well as many others to pray to in time of need. The prayers of Indi-yi-yahn had always been answered, that is, all but the last time.

Slowly Duke Bowman raised his head. The lamplight shone on the baldness of it; the freckled expanse of taut, shiny, dry skin that had once been thatched with bluish, iron-gray hair, the shade of the finest high-carbon steel. Slowly the big man turned to face the slight draft that had suddenly blown into the room from an opened window.

The shadowy figure in the corner spoke softly: "What do you see in the color painting of the embers, Duke?"

"Who are you?" demanded Duke.

Lee held out his left hand so that the lamplight shone on the silver button he held.

"Where did you get this?" asked Duke.

"From an anonymous legal gentleman in Fort Davis who padded this button with a thousand dollars in cash."

Duke looked toward the closed door.

"The house is cold and empty," said Lee. "There is only a woman in the old log *casa*— Stella Dakin."

"The others are hunting for you, eh, Kershaw?"

"They're hunting in the wrong places."

"Vicente Galeras brought you here?"

"He's dead. They killed him at Tinaja del Muerto." Lee held out his other hand to show the silvered cross. "Proof," he said. He opened

27

the velvet-covered photograph case. "And this," he added.

"Did the others see that photograph?"

"Not while I was around."

"How did you get in here?"

"Through North Pass."

"From Tinaja del Muerto at *this* time of the year?"

"I'm here," said Lee simply.

"No one saw you?"

"Only a dog outside. He's in the river now."

Lee came closer to the old man. "I haven't much time," he said. "The wolves may soon be gathering outside. What do you want of me?"

"To do something for me which I can no longer do myself. You see the change in me. You may know of the change in my old *corrida*. Vicente Galeras was the last of the loyal ones working for me."

"And lies in an unmarked grave because of it. Where are the others?"

"Driven one by one from the Broken Bow by the Dakins. Some of them are still in the valley, *beyond* the limit of my range. One by one, Kershaw, until I found myself alone here, a prisoner of the Dakins, while they wait for me to die."

"I'm all sorrow," said Lee drily.

"I want you to find the boy in that photograph. You have your first week's fee. I'll double your usual five hundred a week fee after that, until you bring the boy here."

"Who is this boy?" asked Lee curiously.

Bowman looked up at Lee. "If he's still alive, he's my only living relative. You saw the woman at the log *casa*. You know her?"

"Stella Dakin. She ran a 'house' in El Paso. They called her The Virgin Mary. Her common-law husband died under mysterious circumstances and left her his money. She was cleared of any charges of his death, but she had to leave El Paso. She served time in the Texas State Prison for blackmail, or extortion."

"When she was released she came here five yeas ago to act as my housekeeper," said Bowman quietly.

"You're joking!"

Bowman shook his head. "Now she claims she's my common-law wife, and so, will inherit the Broken Bow."

"Can she make the claim stick?"

"She is a fine-looking woman," replied Bowman. "It was lonely here in this big house. You understand?"

"You always were a lusty man, Bowman."
Lee formed a mental picture of Stella Dakin.
Broad of hip and thin of lip; powerful breasts
divided from a heavy rump and strong legs by
a too tiny waist that gave her body the appear-
ance of a spider; mouth like a tight seam over
tiny pearly teeth; great blue eyes that easily
drew a man to her, until he realized it was not
depth of character in those cerulean orbs but
rather an emptiness of soul into which he was
looking. "The Black Widow," added Lee.
"What about the boy, Bowman?"

"He's my illegitimate son, Bart. A bastard, if
you will."

"What about the lovely woman with him in
the photograph? Was she his sister?"

"His mother rather. She was Rafaela Diaz.
She was nineteen years old when that picture
was taken with the son of whom she was very
proud. She came here as my housekeeper when
she was fifteen years old."

"That was a mistake on her part," said Lee
drily.

"I talked her into my bed and bulled her the
first night she was under my roof. But I had
actually bought that girl, Kershaw. She was a
genizaro—a mixed-blood."

30

"The Heirs of Sorrow. The Children of Many Bloods. From the *Valle de Lagrimas*—the Valley of Tears," softly added Lee.

"She had been captured by the Mescaleros and sold to the Comancheros, who, in turn, sold her to me. She was a virgin, surprisingly enough."

"Where is she now?"

"Dead for eighteen yeas. Murdered by the Mescaleros at the Massacre of Cinco Castillos."

"And the boy?"

"There were persistent rumors for years that there had been one survivor—a small boy of three or four years of age carried off by the Mescaleros. Some years later that button was sent to me by an old priest who lived in Santa Fe. He suggested that the boy might still be alive."

"Did you make an effort to find out?"

It was very quiet in the tower room. An ember snapped in the fireplace. There was a sudden rushing of wind through the *bosque*.

"It didn't matter in those days," said Bowman at last.

"And you base your claim that the boy might still be alive on that silver button sent to you by an old priest many years ago?"

31

"There are no other buttons like that in the world! His mother was clever with her hands. She had cast them herself. She had the photograph taken just before she left here to travel north to show her son to her relatives up north of Santa Fe, near Las Trampas I think it was. They stopped at Cinco Castillos, and she died there."

"You let them travel north when the Mascaleros were on the war path?"

"I thought they were safe enough. Marsh Dakin rode with them, with an escort of some of my best *vaqueros*. They turned back just before the Mescaleros attacked Cinco Castillos."

"Very convenient," murmured Lee.

"Look, Kershaw—I must find my son! He'd be a man now, fit to stand beside his father to take over the Broken Bow."

Lee placed the photograph, the button, and the thousand dollars on the table. "I can't cross into the Land of Shadows to find a boy who vanished eighteen years ago."

"He may still be alive!"

"Forget it, old man. Keep your memories of a child-woman and of a sad-eyed little boy who never knew his own father." Lee turned away.

The crisp double-clicking of a pistol hammer

being cocked stopped Lee in his tracks. "Turn around," ordered Bowman.

Lee turned with his hands raised to shoulder height. "Why?" he asked.

"The Dakins know I sent for you, but they don't know *why* I sent for you. I don't intend to have them find out."

"Your secret is safe with me."

Bowman shook his head. "Not if they catch you."

"They won't," said Lee.

"You can't get out of this valley alive unless I tell you how to do it."

"I'll risk it."

"You might, but *I* won't risk letting you try."

Lee eyed the grim old tyrant. "You really believe that boy is alive and grown into a man?"

"I *have* to believe it!"

"Would he even remember you?"

"Why not?"

"I have the feeling his mother took him from here and never intended for them to come back."

Lee's words seemed like a blow across the old man's face.

33

"Kershaw," he said, "will you try to find him?"

Lee shrugged. "Supposing I do? If I try to bring him back here, the Dakins will kill him, and maybe me, to keep him from getting in to see you. Why don't you turn to the law, Bowman?"

"Who would believe my word against the Dakins'? They've spread stories that I'm senile. If the law tried to find the boy and bring him back here to me, as I want you to do, the Dakins would stop at nothing to kill him."

"What makes you think I can do any better?"

"You're Lee Kershaw," replied Bowman. It was all he said, as though those three words had resolved the whole problem.

"I can hardly refuse after that," said Lee drily. He looked at the dusty medicine shirt hanging on the wall. "Who led the raid on Cinco Castillos?" he asked.

"Indi-yi-yahn."

"Did he know your woman and your son were there at the time?"

Bowman shrugged. "¿Quien sabe? Why?"

"It would have been sweet vengeance," said Lee.

34

"He would have killed the boy then, as well as the woman."

Lee shook his head. "His vengeance would have been greater to raise the son of Duke Bowman as a Mescalero, maybe with the idea that some day the son of Duke Bowman might become the instrument of his revenge on you."

"You talk like you read books!" scoffed Bowman.

Lee smiled. "I might have expected an answer like that." He reached up and took down the medicine shirt, which left a pale ghost of itself against the dusty wall.

"What do you intend to do with that?" asked Bowman.

Lee helped himself to two bottles of brandy from a liquor cabinet and a handful of Bowman's prime and clear Havanas. He rolled the shirt about the liquor bottles and cigars. "Diabolito is the present chief of the Mescaleros. He is the only son of Indi-yi-yahn. Rumor has it that his power is slowly being unsurped by a rising young killer by the name of Baishan who has had a medicine shirt made for him that is supposed to make any other medicine shirt of the Mescaleros look like a cheap copy made in Kansas City for the tourist trade. Now, if

35

Diabolito gets back the shirt of his father, he might very well talk business with me about what happened to your missing son."

"You're loco! They'll kill you on sight! What if they think the power of this shirt was lost when I killed Indi-yi-yahn? If that is so, mister, you'll look damned foolish standing there with a sickly grin on your face holding a dusty hunk of fawnskin painted with crazy symbols and stained with the dried blood of Indi-yi-yahn. It'll turn out to be your death warrant!"

"How do I get out of this death trap?"

"These mountains are pure limestone. The Mescaleros used to claim a man could walk underground through the caves for seventy-five miles from one end of the range to the other. Go up the canyon of the Broken Bow until you see a rockfall on the right hand side. There are three cave entrances there, but only one of them goes all the way through. You'll come out north of here, on the slopes this side of North Pass. For God's sake! Pick the right cave, Kershaw, or you'll never be seen again!"

"How will I know which is the right one?"

"The middle one," replied Bowman. He hesitated. "No, it must be the right-hand one as you face the rock wall."

"Great," murmured Lee.

"You'll have to walk out of the mountain," said Bowman. "You can't get a horse in there."

Lee shook his head. "I left my dun at Ribbon Creek, picketed back in a box canyon, and walked in here."

"You've got more luck than brains. The exit of the right cave will bring you out on the heights above the creek."

Lee studied the old man. "How do I know you're telling me the truth, Bowman? You might want to get rid of me after all."

"There was only one other person who knew about that cave. That was Vicente Galeras. That was how he got out of here under the noses of the Dakins and walked down to Tinaja del Muerto. There was no other way he could have gotten out of here."

Lee shrugged. "I'll have to buy it then." He walked to the window. He looked back at the old man. "When did you start to fail, Bowman?" he suddenly asked.

"About two or three years past. Why do you ask?"

"The change is remarkable. Who cooks your meals?"

Bowman was surprised. "Stella," he replied. "Why?"

Lee thrust a leg through the window.

"Wait, damn you!" snapped Bowman with his old fire. "Don't start something you can't finish! Why did you ask me that?"

Lee looked back from the shadows into the pool of light from the fireplace and the lamp. The lamplight shone on the taut, dry skin of the balding head and the lifeless gray hair that fringed it. He looked into the dull eyes of the old man, aged too much for his time. He looked down at the limp hands on the arms of the chair.

"Tell me, Kershaw," the old man quietly asked.

"Do you know how Stella Dakin lost her first common-law husband?"

"You said mysterious circumstances, Kershaw." The old man looked quickly at the closed door. "Someone has opened the lower door," he said. He looked again at Lee. "Well?" he asked.

"Suspicion of slow arsenic poisoning," said Lee quietly.

The dull eyes looked steadily at Lee. "Yes," Bowman agreed. "*I see it now.* Kershaw, for

God's sake, find my son and bring him back to me before I die!"

A footstep sounded on the tower stairway.

When Bowman peered into the shadows near the window, all he could see was the faded curtain moving in the night breeze that was creeping timorously into the musty room.

The door swung open. "Are you asleep, Duke?" asked Stella.

Duke shook his head.

"Vicente Galeras has left the Broken Bow," she said.

"It doesn't surprise me. He was the last one left of the old New Mexicans who once served me. He's left before. He'll come back."

"Not this time. He was ambushed and killed at Tinaja del Muerto."

"By Mescaleros?"

"No. By a man named Lee Kershaw. You knew him."

"Years ago."

"A paid killer. A bounty hunter."

Duke looked up into her hard face. "Who would pay to have old Vicente Galeras killed?"

"He had enemies."

"They were *my* enemies, not his."

She shrugged. She looked up at the ghostly

light-colored area where once the shirt of Indi-yi-yahn had hung. "The boys are out hunting down Kershaw," she said. "Marsh told me to tell you not to worry—they'd find him."

Bowman laughed.

"What happened to that filthy shirt that used to hang up there?"

"I finally burned it. You've asked me enough times to do so."

She sniffed the musty air. She parted the drapes of the front window and looked down on the dark rushing river with its ghostly swirlings of foam riding the surface. "But why now?" she asked over her shoulder.

"Godalmighty, woman! Do I have to account to you for everything I do!"

"It's time for bed," she said resignedly.

"Mine or yours," he asked bitterly.

"You left *my* bed, Duke," she said.

"You never owned a bed in this damned house! You don't own a damned thing here! The clothes on your back are mine! The food you eat is mine!"

"Yes, Duke," she patiently agreed. She flicked her blue eyes about the room. Something else was missing. Something she had felt a few days before but had not been able to put a finger of thought on. There was a desk in one corner. She reached over to turn out the lamp, and as she did so, she tilted the shade a little. The lamplight touched the desk. Then she knew. The faded velvet-covered photograph case which had once stood there was now missing. She looked quickly at the bare place on the wall where the medicine shirt had once hung, and a piece of the jigsaw puzzle in her mind slipped easily into place. She turned off the lamp.

The door closed behind them. Their footsteps sounded on the stairs. The botton door was opened and closed.

Lee Kershaw stepped back in through the window. He quickly searched the desk and found some fat-bodied candles and some packets of lucifers. He parted the drapes of the front window. Horsemen were on the river road riding toward the *estancia*. He catfooted across the room and out through the window. He crossed the flat roof and dropped lightly into the shrubbery at the base of the wall. He picked up his Winchester and passed noiselessly into the deep shadows of the *bosque* just as many hoofs clattered on the graveled road that led past the great limestone house to the older log buildings.

6

THE sound of angry voices came to Lee from near the old log casa. Lee came up behind the barn and fattened a deep shadow just around the corner from the knot of Dakins standing beside the corral.

"I tell you he was here!" shrilled Stella.

"He ain't in the valley," argued Cass. "He went southwest from Tinaja del Muerto. Didn't he, Nuno?"

Nuno was careful. He was always careful on disagreeing with Cass Dakin. He had a healthy fear of the big man's fists. "It is possible," murmured Nuno.

"Why don't you ask *me*, Cass?" put in Chisos Martin. "I still say he made it to North Pass and crossed over to this side."

"We didn't see any signs of him at Ribbon Creek," said Sid Dakin.

"You won't find any signs of him anywhere," said Marsh Dakin. "Stell, what makes you so damned sure he was here?"

"I went up to get the old man to go to bed.

That filthy old medicine shirt is missing from the wall. The photograph of that breed woman he used to sleep with and her bastard son is missing from his desk. He claims he burned the medicine shirt. Well, I've been after him for months to do that."

"So what the hell has this to do with Kershaw being here?" demanded Cass.

"Why *tonight*?" asked the woman.

"I don't get it yet," said Cass.

"You never will," said Marsh. "Go on, Stell."

"I think I know now why he sent for Kershaw, Marsh. It wasn't to help him against us. Kershaw doesn't get mixed up in this kind of business. He hunts men."

"So?" asked Sid.

It was very quiet for a moment. "Or boys that have grown up into men," added the woman.

"Such as?" asked Marsh.

"Don't you get it?" she demanded. "That loco old man sent for Kershaw to find his son —the kid that was taken by the Mescaleros eighteen years ago at Cinco Castillos."

"You been at the bottle again, Stell?" asked Sid.

"Shut up!" she snapped. "Put two and two together. Isn't it possible that he thinks his son is still alive?"

"He's dead," said Cass.

"A lot you know," put in Marsh. "By God! That just might be the old man's game."

"So what does the medicine shirt have to do with it?" asked Cass.

"If the Mescaleros took the kid with them, and he's still alive, living up in them damned mountains with them, Kershaw would have to have some means of getting in there to talk with the Mescaleros," said Marsh thoughtfully.

"He is mad!" cried Nuno.

"You should be so mad," said Chisos.

"The medicine shirt was missing tonight," added Stella. "The photograph was missing a couple of days ago. Odds are that Duke sent Vicente Galeras with the photograph to show to Kershaw at Tinaja del Muerto."

"I killed the cholo!" shouted Cass. "He never had a chance to talk with Kershaw!"

"Did you search Galeras' body after you killed him?" asked Stella.

It was quiet again. Feet scuffled on the hard ground.

45

"You didn't, did you?" demanded the woman.

"I can't think of everything," blurted Cass.

"You can't think of anything!" she shrilled. "Now you men get to hell out after Kershaw! All the time you're standing here he's moving and moving fast!"

"The man is not human," said Nuno Mercado gloomily. "He can do things no living man can do."

"Well, I'll admit he got into the valley somehow," said Marsh, "but he ain't going to get out of it so easy. Sid, you take Chisos, Cass, and Nuno north to Ribbon Creek. Take an extra horse apiece. If you see him, you may have to ride him down. Take extra canteens and food for a couple of days. Reata, you take some of the boys and head east down the valley toward the Pecos. Sid, if you don't see him, head north as fast a you can toward Cinco Castillos. That's the next waterhole north of Ribbon Creek, and that's where the kid vanished eighteen years ago."

"Loco," said Sid. "That's a trip into hell this time of year."

"¡Vámonos!" yelled the woman.

Horses were saddled. Booted men tramped back and forth. Hoofs rattled on the gravel.

"Two hundred dollars to the man who cuts him down!" yelled Marsh.

The hoofbeats died away in the distance. Lee turned to go.

"They'll have to kill him," the woman said suddenly.

Lee peered around the side of the barn in time to see Marsh light the cigarette in the woman's thin-lipped mouth. He saw the great blue eyes in the flare of the match like chips of glacier ice and with about the same amount of soul in them.

"Why didn't you go with them?" she asked Marsh.

"I'm going to take a look around here," he said as he lighted his own cigarette. The flare of the match showed the sme color of eyes as Stella's, but smaller, though not any harder.

"Why?" she asked. "Are you afraid for me?"

Marsh laughed. "Not ever, Stell! You'd be a match for Kershaw any day. No. I'm going to take a look up the river canyon. Galeras somehow got out of this valley right under our noses. He didn't take a horse. He legged it to Tinaja del Muerto, but he didn't leg it through

47

the pass or over the mountains on either side of the pass. There's a secret way out of here, Stell. I think the old man knows it and so did Galeras. The old man maybe told Kershaw."

"Maybe we can make the old man talk."

"No! We can't risk having him die on our hands. I don't want any investigation made around here."

"Wouldn't that settle the whole problem?"

"Not if Kershaw gets loose and finds Bowman's bastard son."

"Do you think the kid is dead, Marsh?"

"I don't know. But we can't risk that either. Kershaw isn't the kind of man who hunts for shadows."

"I agree. We'll have to keep after him until we kill him. If he does find Bowman's son, we'll have to kill the both of them to keep them from getting back here. We've got no other choice, Marsh. There's too much at stake."

Lee faded into the deep shadows behind the barn as Marsh levered a round into the chamber of his Winchester.

The river rushed along inches from Lee's moccasined feet as he felt his way along the rocky trail that seemed tacked to the side of the dark canyon. Beetling limestone cliffs hung over

Lee's head. Lee looked back down the canyon. A tall man was picking his way over the great log that spanned the river.

Lee crossed the rock fall and scanned the dark wall of limestone. He turned his head and quickly stepped behind a huge tip-tilted slab of limestone that had fallen close to the cliff base. A tall man stood at the edge of the rockfall looking up the narrowing gut of the canyon. He scrambled down the loose slope and stood not five feet away from Lee. He rolled a cigarette and lit it, completely unaware of the man who stood almost within touching distance, with a hand resting on the hilt of his knife.

Marsh studied the dark canyon. The alternate flaring up and dying down of the cigarette tip lit his hard blue eyes and then let them drift into shadow. Finally Marsh flicked his cigarette butt into the foaming river and scrambled back up the rock fall.

Lee passed a hand behind himself into emptiness. He lit a candle and thrust it ahead of him into the cave entrance. He walked slowly forward. Something made him stop. He lowered the candle to see a yawning hole stretching perhaps thirty feet ahead of him into the inner darkness. The faint sound of swiftly rushing water came from the dark pit.

Lee left the cave. He tried another opening and got a hundred feet within it to light a mass of fallen rock that blocked the way. The third attempt found him in a twisting, smooth-floored passage that was cool and had an astringent odor to it. He walked into a large, domed cavern and held up the candle. The flickering light reflected from sparkling bunches of gypsum crystals on the ceiling and the walls and from iciclelike stalactites. The light shone on an emerald-hued pool of clearest water.

At the far side of the domed cavern, he picked up a stale cigarette butt. He sniffed it. "Lobo Negro," he said. Vicente Galeras had passed that way on his one-way trip to death at Tinaja del Muerto.

Lee lighted one of Duke Bowman's clear Havanas to celebrate the occasion. By the time the cigar had burned down to a butt, he felt a cool draft strong on his face. After a little while, he blew out the candle. There was a subtle difference in the darkness ahead of him. He felt his way along the passage, testing the way with the butt of his rifle. In a short time, he stepped out on the northeastern side of the great humped and rounded limestone ridge that extended northward to the shallow pass through which he had traveled on his way to Ribbon Creek.

He watered the dun in the darkness just before the false dawn.

The dun raised its head and slanted its ears toward the southeast. The dawn wind brought the sound of hoofbeats from the lower slopes. Two shadows—that of a tall, lean, moccasined man and that of a rawhide-booted dun—vanished into the thick brush and scrub trees to the north of Ribbon Creek on the way to Cinco Castillos.

7

THE five naked pinnacles of rock thrust themselves up from the flat desert floor like the outspread fingers of a warning hand held palm outward toward the traveler. The pre-moon darkness shielded the base of the pinnacles and the eroded ruins of Cinco Castillos. Beyond the pinnacles rose the towering wolf-fanged mountains—the citadel of the Mescaleros.

Lee Kershaw padded through the darkness with his Winchester at hip level, cocked and ready for rapid fire. The dun was ground-reined in the darkness behind him.

The low-mounded graves of the massacre victims were marked in the darkness by pale, sun-bleached crosses whose lettering had long ago been erased by wind-driven sand. There were thirteen of them.

"There were no survivors," the mind voice murmured.

A feeling of utter loneliness came over Lee. Beyond the ruins and the graves was the base of the five pinnacles, as though five fat and dripping candles had let their wax run freely to congeal in thick masses about their bases. A man-made passage had been cut through the rock to allow access to the shallow rock pans, or *tinajas*, which somehow, miraculously, held water even through the great heat of the summer droughts.

Lee's soft footfalls echoed in the dark passage. He saw the faint glistening of the water. He knelt beside the first *tinaja* and cupped the water up with his free hand, keeping his eyes on the alert. The water stung his cracked lips and ran into his dry mouth and throat. Some of it ran down from his hand and dripped onto his sweat-soaked shirt and through it to his chest. Jesus, but it was good!

He stood up suddenly and whirled, thrusting forward his Winchester toward the mouth of the passageway. Nothing moved. There was an eerie, deathlike stillness about the haunted place.

He climbed a rocky pathway to stand between two of the pinnacles to look toward the south and east where the road from the Rio Penasco was first being lit by the rising moon.

Nothing moved; no thread of dust stained the moonlight.

The moonlight touched the ruins. It lit up the eastern sides of the roofless, eroded buildings and cast their western sides into deep shadow against the light-colored caliche soil. It etched the shapes of the tilted crosses against the mounded soil of the graves.

Lee was alone at Cinco Castillos. He whistled sharply for the dun and walked down the rocky path to meet him. He unsaddled the dun as it drank. He rubbed him down and let him drift over to graze on a meager patch of dried grasses caught in a shallow pocket of drift soil. The dun had eaten the last of Lee's supply of oats the day before.

Lee kindled a fire. He opened out the three collapsible legs of his spider and placed it over the embers. He poured in the last of his bacon fat. When it sizzled, he placed the last of his hard *bizcocho* in the deep fat and then tastefully draped the last of his *carne seca* over the biscuits. He whistled the "Sago Lily" as he basted the hard, dried meat and biscuits.

The dun suddenly raised his head and slanted his ears toward the passageway, Lee turned, automatically reaching for his rifle. His hand was arrested in the motion.

A small figure stood in the mouth of the passage-way.

Lee slowly stood up.

The figure was that of a boy of perhaps three of four years of age wearing a little gray *charro*-type jacket fastened with six large silver buttons.

It was very quiet except for the busy sizzling of the fat.

"I can't cross into the Land of Shadows to find a boy who vanished eighteen years ago," Lee had told Duke Bowman.

"I'm hungry, señor," the small boy said in Spanish.

"Forgive the little one, señor," a rusty-voiced old man said from within the mouth of the pass-ageway. "Our burros strayed this afternoon and took our food with them."

"Come out into the moonlight," ordered Lee.

An old man came out into the moonlight. He held out his work-gnarled hands to show that he was unarmed. He took off his heavy sombrero and revealed a face wrinkled like a hide that has lain too long in the sun. "Cande-lario Melgosa, *servidor de usted*," he said in the old-fashioned courteous manner. "The boy is my great-grandson, Basilio," he proudly added.

Lee nodded. "Your servant," he countered. He would not give his name.

The old man looked past Lee. "The food will soon burn," he politely suggested.

Lee took the spider from the fire. "There is plenty for all," he said. "Come and eat."

Lee was immediately struck by the resemblance of the boy to that of another small boy who had vanished from that very place eighteen years past. He served the food in equal portions. "How long have you been here?" he asked.

"Since before the dawn. We came from the north last night to avoid the heat of the day. While we slept, the burros strayed."

"They will come back for the water. What are you doing here?"

"We come from a village near Las Trampas, in the mountains to the north of Santa Fe. My wife, Filomena, was one of those who died here in the massacre eighteen years ago to this very day. Every year since then, I have come here on this date. This is the first year I have brought the boy. I am very old, you understand, and may not be able to come next year; so I brought the boy with me so that he might know where his great-grandmother lies."

"You came that great distance through the desert in the heat and at a time of drought with this little one?"

"On such a pilgrimage, señor, one does not feel hardships."

"And the Mescaleros? One does not fear them?"

The old man shrugged. "God protected us."

Lee finished his food and fashioned two cigarettes. He placed one in the mouth of the old man and lit both cigarettes. "*Una copita?*" asked Lee, holding a thumb tip and first finger tip about two inches apart. "*Mil gracias,*" murmured the old man. "*Por nada,*" responded Lee as he poured the brandy.

Canderlario sipped the fiery brandy. "You are travelling north?" he asked.

"I go to the mountains from here."

"But the Mescaleros, señor!"

"I have business there."

The old man looked quickly at the dozing boy.

Lee picked up the boy. "The boy is safe, *viejo*. I am not a Comanchero." He placed a blanket on a smooth patch of sand and put Basilio on it. He came back to the fire. "Your wife was traveling through here at the time of the massacre?"

Candelario shook his white head. "In those days, this place was a swing station for the stagecoach line that ran through here before the railway was built farther to the west. I was head hostler then, and my wife was the cook."

Lee lowered his cup from his mouth. "You were here at the time of the massacre?" he asked incredulously.

"I had gone to hunt stray mules. Just before the true dawn, I saw the gun flashes and heard the screaming of the people. I hid near the road and saw the last of the killing."

"So you really are a lone survivor."

"When the Mescaleros left, I buried the bodies."

"Thirteen?" asked Lee.

"Count the graves, señor. Of course, there was the little boy who was taken away by the Mescaleros."

Lee showed the photograph to Candelario. "Him?" he asked.

"I never saw the boy. He came here when I was gone."

"The woman? You recognize her? She died here."

Candelario looked at Lee. "What do you wish to know about her?" he quietly asked.

"I am hunting for the boy of this photograph."

"After eighteen years? Why?"

"I am paid to do such things. Tell me about the woman."

"She was hardly more than a girl. I found her wounded under a pile of the dead. I treated her wound and nursed her back to health."

"You are a *curandero*?"

"You know of the *Penitentes*?" asked Canderlario.

"I know of the *Penitentes*," admitted Lee.

"I am the *Enfermero* of my *morada*. I care for the sick members."

"Go on," urged Lee.

"When she came out of the fever, she cursed the men who had left her and the boy to the hands of the Mescaleros."

"Who were they?"

"They had brought the woman and the boy here while I was gone, and then they had left to return to the Rio Penasco. Before God, señor! They must have heard the shooting and the screaming of the unfortunates here, but they would not return. Had they done so, they could have saved most of the lives of those who were slaughtered here."

"But you don't know who they were?"

"Only their brand. It was on the mules they drew the buggy in which the woman and the boy had been riding. The Mescaleros stole the horses from here, but they slaughtered the mules, for they love the sweet mule meat. I saw the hides of the mules. The brand was plain on their flanks, so . . ." Here Candelario traced a Running MB brand on the fine sand.

"And you never heard of the boy again?"

"Who knows? He may have been killed later. He may have been traded or sold to another tribe. He may have been ransomed. It is also possible that he was raised as a Mescalero and now lives in those mountains."

"And the woman? What happened to her?"

"She had me dig a grave for her and fill it with the bones of one of the mules, as a bitter gesture I think. I made a cross for it with her name on it—Rafaela Diaz, it was. I took her north with me when I returned to my village."

"Where is she now?"

Candelario shrugged. "She left the village

shortly after we returned there. She went to Santa Fe. I never saw her again." Candelario studied Lee. "This lost boy, what does he mean to you?"

"A thousand dollars a week," murmured Lee.

"I do not understand."

Lee stood up. "Sometimes I don't either. I'll round up your burros. When the moon is down, take the boy from this haunted place. Travel during the night and hide out during the day until you are safe from the Mescaleros."

Lee rode past the mounded graves. The names of the crosses were long gone. Which one of them held only the bones of a mule?

The burros were not far from the ruins. Lee drove them toward Cinco Castillos. He looked to the south across the moonlit desert. Dust was rising thinly on the Rio Penasco Road. The fine field glasses picked out the shapes of three horsemen leading three other horses.

Lee drove the burros clattering into the passageway. He dismounted. "You'll have to leave right now, *viejo*," he said. "There are men coming here looking for me, and I don't want them to find me here, or you either, for they will make you talk. Get the boy out of here.

Ride around behind the pinnacles, keeping them in between you and the men who are coming here. Do not raise any dust!" Lee thrust a pair of cigars into the old man's shirt pocket. "Keep moving until it is dark again. Rest, and push on later before the coming of the dawn."

Candelario placed the dozing boy in his saddle and passed a rope about him to hold him there. He led the three burros through the passageway. Lee followed him, leading the dun. "Remember!" he called out. "No dust, *viejo*!"

Lee led the dun, around the opposite side of the pinnacles and ran lightly, leading the trotting dun. He kept the pinnacles always between him and the Rio Penasco Road until he reached lower ground, out of sight of the ruins, where he mounted and rode steadily toward the distant moonlit mountains.

8

NUNO MERCADO kicked through a pile of fresh manure. "There was someone just here," he said over his shoulder.

"Mescaleros," said Cass.

"It was an oat-fed horse," said Nuno. "Mescaleros graze their horses. White men feed them oats."

Chisos pressed a hand down on the sand that covered the fire ashes. "Still warm," he said.

"From the sun," said Cass.

Chisos kicked at the sand and ashes. A smoking ember landed near Cass. "Some sun," said Chisos drily.

"Mescaleros," insisted Cass.

Nuno shook his head. "They never come here. Not for eighteen years. They fear the ghosts of the slaughtered."

"Superstitious bull," said Cass.

"Perhaps," agreed Nuno. "But *they* believe it." Nuno climbed the rocky path to stand between two of the pinnacles. "There is dust

63

rising on the road to the north!" He plunged recklessly down to get his horse.

"Dust devil," said Cass.

Chisos led his horse at a run toward the passage. "There ain't no wind!" he yelled back.

Out on the road to the north, Candelario Melgosa looked back at the satisfactory cloud of dust he had raised by dragging a blanket behind his burro. He drew in on the rope and folded the blanket over his cantle as he heard the sound of many hoofbeats approaching from the south.

Chisos dismounted at a run. "Stay right there old man," he ordered.

Candelario politely raised his sombrero. "I was not planning to go on, señor," he said.

Nuno dismounted and looked incredulously at the old man, the little boy, and the three dusty, little, two-dollar burros. "Before God, *viejo*," he said. "What do you do out here on the desert at night?"

"I avoid the heat of the day, señor."

"You were just at Cinco Castillos?"

Candelario nodded. "I cooked a meal there."

Cass rode up and dismounted heavily. He looked hard at the old man. "Your burros crap back there?" he asked.

Candelario smiled. "They have good bowel movements, señor."

"Don't get funny!" Cass looked triumphantly at Nuno. "See?"

"You think this old *paisano* has enough pesos to feed his burros oats?" asked Chisos.

"What were you doing at Cinco Castillos, *viejo*?" asked Nuno.

"I was visiting the grave of my wife, Filomena, who died there in the massacre eighteen years ago this very day."

"Was there anyone else there?" asked Chisos.

"I saw no one," lied Candelario.

Nuno looked at Chisos. "Maybe Kershaw went west instead of north from Ribbon Creek, eh?"

Chisos shook his head. "He had to come here for water." He reached over and plucked two cigars from the shirt pocket of Candelario. He sniffed at them and read the bands in the bright moonlight. "By God!" he said. "These are the Duke's private brand!" He gathered together the front of the old man's jacket and drew him close. "Now, you old bastard," he threatened, "you just tell us about the big gringo who was just back there at Cinco Castillos."

Candelario slanted his eyes to the west. A

faint thread of dust showed rising in line with the mountains. "A tall man with reddish hair, short beard, and a big nose, and gray eyes that were cold, but showed warmth when he looked at my great-grandson. He rode a fine dun, a *tostado*—a beautiful horse, señores."

Cass ambled over to look down at the frail little man. "Where did he go?" he demanded.

"I don't know." Candelario slewed his eyes to look west. It was a fatal mistake. Cass turned and saw the thread of dust. He whirled. "You old bastard!" he yelled. "You were holding us here to give him time to get away!" He hit the old man once, a heavy solid blow like a butcher slamming his cleaver through a thick joint of meat. Candelario fell to the dust of the road and lay there with his neck bent at an awkward angle and with his eyes staring up at the man who had killed him.

Nuno crossed himself. He knelt beside the old man and went through his pockets. "Damn!" he said. "Not a centavo!"

Cass plucked one of the cigars from Chisos' hand. He lit it. "What the hell did you expect?" he asked around the cigar.

"He's heading for the mountains," said Chisos.

"And maybe the Mescaleros," added Nuno.

"Why?" asked Cass.

"He has the shirt of Indi-yi-yahn," said Chisos.

"Maybe they'll bury him in it," suggested Cass.

"There's more to it than that," mused Chisos. "He came here for information on the kid and the woman that were here eighteen years ago."

"He came here for water," said Cass.

Chisos nodded. "*And* information," he insisted.

"You think he's still hunting for the boy who was here eighteen years ago?" asked Nuno.

"That's what Stella thinks," said Chisos.

"Well," said Cass, "I, for one, ain't goin' up in them mountains after him, and to hell with Stella!"

Chisos shrugged. "If there is one man who can go up in them mountains and come out of them again, it's likely him."

"Bull!" snapped Cass. "I ain't goin' to sit around and wait for him."

"He might make it," suggested Nuno. "And if he does, he'll go on looking for the old man's son."

"Where's the next waterhole north, Nuno?" asked Chisos.

"Just to the northwest of the mountains. There are old ruins there, abandoned by the padres many years ago. If Kershaw comes down out of those mountains, that is where he'll have to go for water."

"He'll never make it," said Cass.

Chisos looked at him. "Ten bucks he does."

Cass rubbed his jaw. He grinned. "One week time limit?" he asked.

"Fair enough. If he doesn't come out of them mountains in a week, he'll never come out of them."

"What about the boy?" asked Nuno.

They all looked at the sober-faced little lad who sat in his saddle looking down at his great-grandfather. Cass dropped his hand to his Colt.

"No," said Chisos.

"You gettin' soft?" sneered Cass.

"That shot could be heard for miles! You want the Mescaleros to know we're out here?"

"I ain't that scared of the Mescaleros!"

"Well, maybe *I* am!"

Cass grinned.

"It is bad luck to kill a child," put in Nuno. "We can turn the burros loose and take the boy

68

with us to the ruins. We can leave him with anyone who passes by."

"Like Kershaw?" jeered Cass.

Nuno looked quickly at the big man. "Why do you say that?" he asked.

"How the hell do I know! Why?"

Nuno crossed himself again. "I don't know," he said. He took the boy and mounted his horse. "What about the old man?" he asked.

"In a week the bones will be picked clean," said Chisos. "The buzzards by day and the coyotes by night."

Nuno watched the two Anglos ride back toward Cinco Castillos. The staring eyes of the old man had begun to unnerve him. He turned his head away and followed the others. A curious foreboding had begun to haunt him.

9

THE evening wind blew softly through the murmuring pines. A stream chuckled as it raced between grassy banks. The new moon was riding high overhead. A great fire crackled and flared in a semicircular clearing against a backdrop of a curved rock formation like the band shell in a public park.

The Mescalero warriors seated on the packed dancing ground formed a semicircle, a continuation of the curved rock formation, the center of which was the great fire. Smoke wreathed upward, and fat pine sparks soared brightly through the smoke.

A faint whistling sound came from the dark shadows within the woods behind the seated warriors. Something moved within the woods. Suddenly and dramatically, as though engendered from the earth itself or compounded from drifting smoke and errant moonbeams, a grotesque figure appeared at the edge of the woods, whirling over its head a pierced and shaped piece of wood whose sound was like that of a rush of rain-laden wind through the great pines themselves. Faster and faster whirled the long leather thong, and the sound of the bullroarer increased so that it carried to the depths of the dark woods. The strange and eerie figure of the *diyi* advanced slowly into the cleared area between the fire and the seated warriors. He wore the traditional medicine shirt of a Mescalero shaman, painted with the mystic symbols of water beetle, spider, sun, moon, stars, lightning, thunder, and rain. The shirt was old, well worn, and greasy to the sight and touch. Upon the *diyi*'s head was a headdress made from a strangled fawn, from which protruded two polished buffalo horns. Under the edge of the headdress, his painted face looked like nothing human.

The *diyi* thrust out a hand toward the fire, and a great flare of reddish smoke swirled upward. He thrust out the hand again, and a glittering shower of *hoddentin*, sparkling mica crystals seemed to explode over the flames.

A warrior began to beat on a stiffened hide with a hooped stick. Here and there among the assembled warriors, some of the younger ones stood up and tied back their thick black hair.

71

They drew the long flaps of their buckskin loin-cloths up through their belts to shorten them. They slung bandoleers of polished brass cartridges about their naked shoulders and chests. They picked up their weapons.

Four young warriors marching abreast, advanced to the fire and circled it four times. Two of them stopped on the north side of the fire, and two of them stopped on the south side. Singers gathered about the hide drummer. The four warriors danced in rhythm, moving toward each other to change sides and then to dance back the other way.

The dancers put cartridges between their strong white teeth and between their strong brown fingers. They swayed violently, dropping down upon one knee and then springing high into the air. Guns flashed and roared. An arrow was loosed through the fire and gun smoke, flashing in the moonlight. It seemed to disappear for a split second as it reached the zenith of its flight and then it turned over, reflecting the cold moonlight from the polished cane shaft and plunging downward to drive deep into the ground.

"*Wah! Wah! Wah!*" The dancers' hoarse

grunting cries echoed through the shadowed woods.

One after another the younger warriors dashed onto the firelit dancing ground and swung into the stomping, pounding rhythm of the war dance. The older warriors did not move. They watched the dancers, and among them was Diabolito, the only son of Indi-yi-yahn, who did not want this war.

The *diyi* ran the show like a ringmaster. "You, Long Ear!" he cried out. "You, Long Ear! Many times you have talked bravely! Now, many brave people are calling to you!"

Long Ear obeyed the summons. He dashed in among the sweating dancers, thrusting his long double-barreled shotgun up and down in time with the heady rhythm.

"You, Yellow Bear!" shrieked the *diyi*. "You, Yellow Bear! There are brave people dancing here who would welcome you!"

Yellow Bear joined the dancers. He flourished his polished lance with all the skill of a drum major.

"Coyote, they say to you! You! You! You! They call you again and again!" cried the *diyi*.

Coyote dashed into the firelight. "Tudevia! Tudevia! Tudevia!" he called back. "You are

73

a man! Now I am calling you! You, Mah-Ko! Mah-Ko! I call to you again and again!"

The scene became reminiscent of hell or the Celts dancing about the Beltane fires. Guns flashed and cracked. Warriors called persistently to those who still watched the dance. Sweat was flung glistening from taut, painted faces.

The drumming suddenly lowered in pitch. The dancers stopped calling.

"Baishan! Baishan! Baishan!" called the *diyi*. "They say to you! You! You! You! They call you again and again!"

A broad-shouldered warrior came trotting easily from the woods and leaped into the dancing circle. The firelight showed warm against his new medicine shirt. The yelling rose to a bloodcurdling pitch as Baishan dominated the dance. His entry had been perfectly timed, and now he was showing his stuff. It would be only a matter of time before he would dash from the firelit area through the woods to the waiting horses and carry the war party down the long mountain slopes to raid, kill, and pillage.

A tall, reddish-bearded man walked easily into the firelight carrying a dusty, folded-up, deerskin shirt of a dingy brownish color, stained with what looked like smears of black paint. A cigar was stuck jauntily in one corner of his mouth, and the bluish smoke wreathed about his lean, bronzed hawk's face with its piercing gray eyes.

The drumming stopped first. The singing died away. One by one the sweating dancers stopped still and stared at the White-Eye who had appeared among them as though summoned by their dancing, and wild chanting, as Baishan himself had been called forth.

The wind moaned a little through the tree tops. The moon was slanting down toward the west. The fire was crackling lower and lower over a thick bed of embers.

No one moved.

Lee walked easily to where Diabolito sat among the older warriors.

Baishan snatched the double-barreled shotgun from the hands of Long Ear. He swept back the hammers with a sharp cut of his left hand. He walked between Diabolito and Lee and pointed the ten-gauge muzzles at the face of the White-Eye. Lee looked into the eyes of Baishan over the barrels of the shotgun. "I came here to talk in peace with Diabolito," said Lee in passable Mescalero. He could not show a mote of fear in his own eyes; to do so would be to die at once with his face missing.

"Wait," said Diabolito to Baishan. "I am still the chief here. Let the White-Eye speak."

Lee slowly raised a hand and pushed the shotgun aside. "I came here, as a man, to talk with a man," he announced. He had put the issue squarely up to Diabolito and the older Mescalero warriors. Was Diabolito still the chief, and not in name only? There was no hereditary line of chieftainship among the Mescaleros. Diabolito had only succeeded his father Indi-yi-yahn because he had been the best warrior in the tribe, not because he was the son of Indi-yi-yahn. Who was the best warrior now! Diabolito or the would-be usurper Baishan?

"I know you now," said Diabolito to Lee. "You came here years ago and fought against us. You are the one called Hunter of Men. The one who can kill so swiftly."

"Can he die as swiftly as he kills?" demanded Baishan. He did not want to lose face in front of this calm white man. The gods had been with him that night up until the very last moment when the White-Eye had appeared, seemingly from nowhere.

Lee walked around Baishan, expecting at any second to hear the double-crashing report of the scattergun and to feel the smashing impact of buck and ball in his back. He watched the eyes of the warriors who looked past him into the taut, painted face of Baishan, hoping he might get a split second warning if Baishan made his killing move.

At the last possible second, Lee suddenly unrolled the bloodstained medicine shirt of Indi-yi-yahn in front of Diabolito. He heard the gasping intake of breath from the older warriors.

"Where did you get this?" asked the chief.

"From the old man of the Broken Bow."

"The shirt means nothing now!" cried Baishan. "Did not your own father go to the Land of Shadows leaving that shirt in the bloody hands of that old devil of the Broken Bow? There is no power left in that shirt! Its medicine is lost!"

Lee slowly turned his head. "And how good is the medicine of your shirt?"

Baishan's face worked. He was no fool. He had always been able to think quicker than his fellows. "The power of that shirt went into that old devil of the Broken Bow. That is so, because we Mescaleros were never again able to challenge his power for that land which is ours."

Lee shrugged carelessly. "How can you prove that?"

"Through this shirt I now wear! It now has the power!"

"The White-Eye asked you how you can prove it. You did not answer him," said Diabolito.

"Let me fight him to the death. If I win, then my shirt has the power. If he wins, then the power is still in the old shirt."

"You think fast for a Mescalero, sonny," said Lee quietly. Baishan had neatly caught Lee's tail in a crack.

Baishan stripped off his medicine shirt and wound it about his left forearm. He unsheathed his knife and drew it lightly across his left bicep to draw blood, which he sucked up and spat at Lee.

Lee felt his face skin tighten and his bowels loosen. "Sweet Jesus," he breathed.

Baishan stood there like a bronze image. Only the sweat moved on his broad chest and bulging muscles.

"You don't have to meet the challenge," suggested Diabolito.

"And if I don't?" asked Lee.

The answer was plain in the eyes of the old chief and on the faces of the warriors. The struggle for power in the tribe had now shifted from Diabolito into the hands of Lee, as the champion of the chief and the older warriors who had opposed the war talk of Baishan, who was backed by the younger hotbloods of the tribe.

Lee dropped his cigar and trod on it. "A thousand a week," he murmured. "I pay my own expenses."

"Do you pray to your god, Hunter of Men?" asked Diabolito.

Lee nodded. "In a sense," he agreed. He stripped off shirt and undershirt to reveal his lean, long-muscled body puckered with bullet holes and with the white cicatrices of old knife wounds scarring the hard flesh.

"I came unarmed," he said.

A knife was thrown at his feet. He picked it up and hefted it, testing the edge with a thumb. It was a cheap trade knife without heft or balance. Diabolito threw his own knife at Lee's feet. It was made in the Mexican fashion of the finest Oaxaca steel and seemed cunningly fitted to the strong hand of Lee Kershaw. He picked up the old medicine shirt and wound it tightly about his left forearm. He turned now to face the waiting Mescalero.

The moon was beyond the mountain now, and long shadows filled the circle; few of the shadows were driven back by the light of the great bed of embers on the hard-packed dancing earth.

Lee drew the razor edge of the knife lightly across his left bicep. He sucked up the blood and spat it at Baishan. "Knife and awl," he flung at Baishan. The words had no meaning of their own. There were no true curse words in the Apache language; the implication of "knife and awl" had been lost in their history, but nothing worse could be said to an Apache.

Lee moved in on the attack. The coaching words of old Anselmo Campos, that master of knife fighting came back to Lee, who had been born and bred a gunfighter: "Try to keep the light in his eyes. A knife fight does not last very long. It does not have the honor and tradition of the duel. An opponent dies slowly with many cuts but swiftly with one that is right. If you cannot kill him at once, weaken

80

him with many small cuts until the chance for the death stroke comes. Above all! Keep calm!"

Lee stopped with his back to the light of the fire, weaving his body back and forth and sideways from the hips, knife partway extended, legs planted apart, balanced on the balls of the feet, and eyes always on the eyes of Baishan.

Baishan tested Lee's reaction. His blade came in high for the face and then dropped low, turning sideways for the swift and fatal disemboweling slash. Lee sucked in his lean gut and moved backward a little. He leaned forward from the hips, and his blade clashed against that of Baishan. The blades went slowly upward, locked together as each man tested the muscular power of the other. They stood there together, straining in the firelight, blade against blade and wrist against wrist in a grim tableau. The blades suddenly went down and sideways. Lee disengaged, and as he did so, he brought the point of his left elbow hard against the right jaw of the Mescalero in a little knife-fighting refinement of his own. Baishan was staggered. Before he could recover, Lee's blade had swept across Baishan's right bicep, drawing forth the blood, bright in the firelight.

Lee retreated. Baishan bulled in. His swift

slash ripped into the deerskin shirt about Lee's left forearm. Lee made no effort to counter strike. Instead, he brought up his knee into Baishan's crotch in a smashing, sickening blow, out of sight of the watching Mescaleros. Lee grinned into Biashan's agonized face. "Cry 'Foul', you sonofabitch," he said. His knife raked a red line across the Mescalero's broad chest.

Baishan retreated. Lee circled around to get the Mescalero's back to the great heat of the thick bed of embers. Baishan slipped sideways so that he stood in the area between the fire and the high rock formation behind the dancing area where the heat had reflected from the rocks.

They closed and fought with the shadow figures aping their every move on the rock face. They leaped in, retreated, swayed sideways and backwards, with the blades clicking and clashing and the sound of their moccasined feet beating a hard tattoo on the packed dancing ground. Again and again, Lee made his small stabbing cuts, followed always by the hard smashing impact of his elbow against the jaw of the Mescalero.

Lee forced Baishan back against the intense heat of the thick bed of embers. The heat seared against the backs of the Mescalero's legs. Lee bored in. Baishan's heels were in the embers. He could not stand the heat. He turned sideways to work his way from the fire. Lee's blade struck at the small of his back.

Baishan whirled. The *heshke* was on him now—the wild killing rage of the Apache, wherein he felt no exhaustion or pain, nothing but the overwhelming desire to kill.

"*Zastee! Zastee! Zastee! Kill! Kill! Kill!*" shrieked the *diyi*.

But Baishan did not meet in combat a modern, civilized, white man, trained to fight with fist, foot, and gun, but rather a transfiguration of a warrior who had gone back into his own Viking-Scots ancestry to match the *heshke* with the *berserker* rage.

They drove at each other like mad bulls; like ripping, tearing, clawing great cats; like leaping, fang-slashing *lobos*. Lee drove Baishan back toward the fire until his heels again rested in the embers. Lee struck at Baishan's face with the knife, and at the last possible instant, he turned his hand sideways so that the big knuckles, taut white in the grip about the hilt of the knife, smashed with stunning force against the sweat-dripping jaw of the Mescalero.

Baishan staggered backward, ankle deep in glowing embers. Despite his Apache training, he shrieked in intense agony. He tried to get out of the embers, only to be met by a grinning devil of a white man who drove him back again. At last, he turned and plowed shrieking through the thick bed of embers toward the watching warriors, scattering the coals to either side, driving hard with the last of his will power to reach the far side.

Lee raced around the great bed of embers. Baishan staggered out of the fire. His moccasins were aflame. His feet were a seared, blistered mass of sheer agony. He could not go back. He charged like a true Mescalero, knowing he was to die, but trying to take his killer with him.

The knife flashed through the firelight and struck deep and hard in the chest of Baishan. He straightened up spasmodically. He swung once with his knife, inches past the sweating face of the white man, and then fell backward into the embers. His medicine shirt flared up, and in the eerie, flickering, flamelight, his staring eyes seemed to come back to life.

Lee dragged the Mescalero from the embers. He turned to look at Diabolito. The chief sat there alone. Only drifting shadows in the deep woods revealed where the warriors had gone. "Will it be peace then?" asked Lee. Diabolito nodded.

Lee walked slowly to the chief. He unwound the medicine shirt if Indi-yi-yahn from his left forearm and gave it to the chief. Lee wiped the sweat from his body and pulled on his undershirt and shirt.

"Why did you really come here, Hunter of Men?" asked Diabolito.

Lee made up two cigarettes. One he placed between the lips of the chief, and the other he placed between his own lips. He thumbsnapped a lucifer into flame and lit the cigarette for Diabolito. "Were there any survivors of the massacre at Cinco Castillos?" he asked around his cigarette as he lit it.

"There was much blood there that day," the chief evasively replied.

"There is a rumor that a small boy was taken here from that place."

Diabolito nodded. "That is so."

"What happened to him?"

"I was not at the massacre of Cinco Castillos. I was in the south, stealing horses from the Nakai-Yes. It was my father who led the raid on Cinco Castillos."

"But the boy must have been here when you returned."

Diabolito was puzzled. "Which boy?" he asked.

Lee showed the photograph to Diabolito. "I am not sure," said the chief. "There were two boys of that age brought here at that time. One from Cinco Castillos. One from up north. He had been captured by the Jicarillas and traded to us for horses. Thus, there were *two* boys here, about the same age. After a time, I could not tell them apart. One of them was ransomed from us by a priest from Santa Fe, to give back to his mother. I was never sure that we let the priest have the right boy."

"And the other small boy?"

"He was raised as a Mescalero."

"Where is he now?"

Diabolito looked at the smoldering body of Baishan. "*There*," he said quietly.

10

IT was a place of ancient ruins under the dreaming moonlight. The roofless church dominated the other smaller buildings. Beyond the ruins across bare flat ground was a great *bosque* of cottonwoods and willows shielding the spring from sight. Beyond the *bosque* was the great, ghastly white expanse of a salt *laguna* that stretched northward for many miles.

Cass Dakin sat on the floor of the church nave playing solitaire in the moonlight that came streaming through the high windows. He looked up at Nuno Mercado perched in the crumbling bell tower. "You see anything, Nuno?" he called up.

"*Nada*," said Nuno.

"He ain't comin', Chisos," said Cass. "I win the bet."

Chisos shook his head. "There's four days to go."

"The Mescaleros got him."

"We should wait," advised Nuno.

"Jesus Christ!" snapped Cass. "You still think he ain't human! Well, he can bleed like the rest of us, and he's likely dead up in them mountains."

"Nothing is impossible for that man," insisted Nuno.

"I'd like to find out with a .44/40 slug," said Cass.

"He is very fast with the guns," warned Nuno.

"Faster than me?" challenged Chisos.

Cass turned over a card. "All right," he said. "We can wait. Go take a look at the horses and the kid, Chisos, and see if they're all right."

"I'll go when I'm ready," retorted Chisos.

The horses grazed in a large enclosure bounded by small cell-like rooms. A lean figure rolled over the wall and landed lightly on its feet. Lee Kershaw catfooted across the enclosure and looked in on little Basilio Melgosa, sound asleep on a horse blanket. Lee picked him up without awakening him. He carried him from the enclosure to a deep draw where the dun stood ground-reined. Lee returned to the enclosure and let the horses drift out onto the open ground where the grazing was thicker. He took his two big canteens and circled far around the ruins to come in toward the *bosque* on the shadowed side.

Chisos Martin looked into the enclosure. He looked into the cell where Basilio had been sleeping. He looked out across the open ground and saw the horses drifting half a mile away. He walked back into the church. "Throw down that pair of tens, Nuno!" he called up.

"The bet was that Kershaw wouldn't be here within the week," reminded Nuno.

Chisos smiled. "That's right," he agreed. "And the sonofabitch got here while we stood around in this damned ruined. He let the horses drift. He took the kid. He's likely in the *bosque* right now gettin' his water."

Nuno looked toward the *bosque*. "The moon is low," he said. "There are thick shadows in the *bosque*."

Cass stood up and reached for his rifle.

"Wait," said Chisos. "I'm aimin' to prove I'm a faster gun that Kershaw."

"That's loco," said Cass. "The three of us can make sure of him."

"Why bother?" asked Chisos. He drew his fine Colt and snapped open the loading gate. He twirled the cylinder to check the loads and then snapped shut the loading gate. He sheathed the sixgun.

"I can hit him from here with the long gun," said Cass.

"You can't even see him," said Chisos.

"We can sweep the *bosque* with slugs."

"Where's your sportin' blood?" jeered the Texan.

"This ain't sport! It's business! You listen to me, Chisos! You're good with the cutter, maybe one of the best, but there's always someone, somewhere, who's faster than you are."

"Marsh offered two hundred dollars for the man who cut down Kershaw. I'd cut my own brother down for that kind of money. Twenty bucks says I take him, Cass."

Cass seemed to have a flash of inspiration; rare indeed for him. He slowly nodded.

Chisos left the church as silently as a hunting cat.

Nuno looked down at Cass. "He shouldn't try Kershaw alone."

Cass grinned. "Why not? If Kershaw kills him, we kill Kershaw."

"And if Chisos kills Kershaw?"

"That Texas punk hasn't been nothing but trouble to me. Now, if he does kill Kershaw, he'll go crowin' back to Marsh to collect his two hundred bucks, which will make me look *very* bad, amigo. But, if I go back to Marsh and tell him it was me that killed Kershaw, I get the credit *and* the two hundred bucks, plus the twenty Chisos bet he could take Kershaw." The low cunning of the stupid showed on his broad face.

Nuno was puzzled. "But if Chisos does kill Kershaw, how can you claim you did it?" He saw the answer on the face of Cass. A cold feeling coursed through his body.

The only sound in the shadowed *bosque* was the metallic whirring of the locusts. Lee glanced toward the moonlit church. Nothing moved. He submerged his canteens in he water.

"Kershaw," the soft Texas voice said from behind Lee.

Lee turned his head. The man was nothing more than a lean shadow close beside the thick bole of a cottonwood. Lee slowly stood up. His rifle was beside his left foot.

"You are Kershaw, aren't you?" asked the Texan.

"You know I am." Lee slanted his eyes toward the church. Something moved in the bell tower. The shadow in a nave window was darker than it should be.

"You move fast. How did you get past the Mescaleros?"

"They like me," Lee drily replied.

"Why?"

"Personality," replied Lee.

"Maybe you're a breed of some kind?"

"We're all breeds of one kind or another— even Texans."

Chisos stepped away from the tree. "They say you're fast with a sixgun."

"I get by," said Lee modestly.

"My two compañeros back there think you might be as fast as me."

"Men of rare judgment," murmured Lee.

"So, I came out here to prove you are not."

"Backed by their rifles?"

"They'll keep out of it."

"As long as you kill me, is that it?"

"Is there a doubt in your mind?"

"How much am I worth in this killing business?"

"Two hundred cash in hand, and worth a helluva lot more in the long run to the Dakins."

"I thought I might be worth more than two hundred."

"Times are hard, Kershaw."

"I'll double that killing fee to let me pass."

Chisos laughed. "When I kill you, I get what's in your wallet, as well as the two hundred."

"And, if you don't kill me, you don't get a cent. But then, it won't make any difference if *you're* dead, will it?"

"You suggestin' that you can kill me?"

"You're getting the idea," admitted Lee.

The locusts had stopped their strident whirring. It was very quiet in the *bosque*—deathly quiet.

"You're in my way, mister," quietly warned Lee.

Chisos calmly nodded.

"Is it a duel you want, Texas? Shall we stand back to back like little Southern gentlemen and pace off ten paces to turn and fire?"

"Just make your play, mister, any time you're ready."

Lee looked quickly sideways. "Looks like one of your rifleman friends is getting ready to beat you to the kill, mister."

Chisos turned his head. Lee's sixgun exploded. The .44/40 slug caught Chisos just below the heart. In the last instant before death,

Chisos realized the stark truth—he'd never known whether or not he was faster than Lee Kershaw.

Lee dropped flat as the shot's echo racketed through the *bosque*. He snatched up his Winchester as he rolled over and over to get behind a tree. He rolled up onto his feet, firing as he arose, working lever and pulling trigger to slam out ten rapid rounds toward the church to keep down the heads of the riflemen. The last of the shots' echoes were rolling along the low hills as Lee ran through the smoke-rifted *bosque*. He plunged into the draw where he had left the dun and the boy. He tucked Basilio under one arm and mounted the dun. He raced toward the drifting horses and stampeded them, driving three of them north toward the glaring, moonlit expanse of the salt *laguna*.

Rifle fire sparkled from the church. One of the driven horses faltered in its stride. Lee was a mile from the ruins when he remembered the two canteens he had left submerged in the spring.

11

CASS DAKIN hooked toe under the body of Chisos and flipped him over onto his back. "Goddamned if I thought Kershaw was faster than Chisos," he said as he knelt beside the body and felt for the Texan's wallet.

"He wasn't," said Nuno quietly.

"He's dead, ain't he?"

"He did not die because Kershaw was faster with a gun. He died because Kershaw was faster with his wits. Did you not see Chisos look away from him a second before Kershaw fired?"

Cass nodded thoughtfully as he counted the bills in the wallet. "Chisos never cleared leather," he said. "Anyway, Kershaw ain't very good with the long gun. He didn't get near us with one of them shots of his."

"Mother of God! The horses!" Nuno legged it from the *bosque*. "They are all gone!" he yelled back a few minutes later.

"They'll come back to the water," said Cass.

Nuno walked back into the *bosque*. "Three

of them are out in the open. He stampeded the other three."

"He must have known all along we were in the church. Yet he come right in here to the *bosque* to get water when the three of us could have gotten him easily with the long guns."

"He had to have the water. It was either that, or turn back, and *nothing* can make *him* turn back, *patrón*."

Cass grinned. "Oh, I don't know. Look there in the spring."

Nuno looked down at the two big blanket-covered canteens submerged in the water. "He will find a way," he prophesied.

"He'll die of thirst out there. Is the boy still here?"

"Kershaw must have taken him with him."

"Go round up them three horses. Kershaw won't get far ahead of us without water. If we keep pushin' him, we'll get him all right."

Nuno walked out of the *bosque*. Far out on the *laguna*, he saw a faint spark of light as Kershaw lighted a cigarette. Nuno crossed himself and went on to get the horses.

Later, in the predawn darkness, Cass Dakin and Nuno Mercado rode along the edge of the salt *laguna*, Nuno leading the spare horse. Cass

96

laughed. "No water," he said. He laughed again.

"Wait, *patrón*," said Nuno. "Look there!" He pointed to a dark hole that showed against the ghostly white surface of the *laguna*. He dismounted and knelt beside the hole. He dipped a hand into the water and tasted it. "Brackish," he said, "but it will keep a man alive." He looked beyond the hole and then walked across the heavily hoof-trampled ground. He thumb-snapped a match into fire and looked down at a gutted horse. He walked back to the water.

"Well?" asked Cass as he shaped a cigarette.

"That man is the devil," avowed Nuno. "Look here! He drove the horses back and forth on the soft ground here at the edge of the *laguna* to raise the water to the surface. He dug his *pozito* just here because he saw the growths along the bank, indicating that there was water deep beneath the surface of the *laguna*. He watered the horses with it when it rose to the surface."

Cass lighted the cigarette. "So? He ain't got any canteens for him and the kid."

"Not so! See there! The dead horse? He gutted it and withdrew the large intestine. He

97

filled it with the water—an Apache canteen! There is enough for him and the boy to make the next waterhole. He will ride the spare horses to death, if he has to, and then shift to the others. He is miles north by now!"

"No white man would drink outa a thing like that," sneered Cass in disgust.

"Kershaw would, *patrón*! I think I will turn back now."

Cass rested an elbow on his saddlehorn and studied the dark face of the New Mexican. "Why?" he asked.

"I have the second sight, *patrón*. One of us will not return from the north. I was born with a caul on my face. I know these things, *patrón*! I have the gift of prophecy."

"You were born in a barnyard with cowshit on your face! Get on that horse!"

"At least we should send back for help!"

"We can telegraph back to the Broken Bow when we get north."

Nuno mounted his horse and reached down to pick up the reins of the spare. He waited until Cass rode on and then he swiftly crossed himself. In a little while, the *laguna* was quite again, just before the coming of the dawn light. A coyote came trotting silently out of the mesquite. He drank daintily from the *pozito* and looked to the north. After a little while, he trotted to the dead horse and began to tear at the guts, left there courtesy of Lee Kershaw.

12

LEE KERSHAW opened one of the ancient, warped double doors of the chapel. The warm spicy odor of burning candles flowed about his face. He looked back over his shoulder. He had lost a day's time in the ride north. A horse had gone lame, and the boy was wearing out. Lee led the boy into the narrow nave. The reredos behind the altar reflected the soft, glowing light of the many candles. The light brought out the lifelike flesh tones of the suffering Christ suspended on his dark cross against the whitewashed wall of the chapel and the bright droplets of blood from the piercing crown of thorns. The chapel seemed empty of life.

"Jesus," said Basilio.

Lee nodded. The faint sound of a mumbling voice came to him. He led the boy to the altar. The kneeling figure of a small-bodied padre was there, with the cowl thrown back from the pure white hair of his head.

"Padre Nicolás?" asked Lee.

The padre slowly turned his head. His dreamlike face seemed made of old ivory that had the lines and wrinkles of ancient parchment on it. The old man got stiffly to his feet. "I am he," he said. "What can I do for you, my son?"

"I was told you would be here. You were once a missionary to the Mescaleros?"

The old man nodded. He looked down at the face of Basilio. "He has the face of a small angel," he said.

"Once you bartered with Indi-yi-yahn, the Mescalero chief, for the ransom of a small boy about the size of little Basilio here. You brought the boy back to his mother here in Santa Fe."

"There were a number of white children for whom I bartered. I was not always successful. One boy, I know, stayed with the Mescaleros and became a warrior. He was named Baishan."

Lee held out the photograph. The padre looked at it dimly. "That might be the boy," he said doubtfully. Lee held out the silver button. "Did he have a jacket with buttons like this?"

The padre eyed the button. "I am not sure."

"You sent this button to the boy's father some years past. To Mark Bowman of the Broken Bow."

"That might be, my son."

Lee was patient. "There were two small boys in the *ranchería* of the Mascaleros at the time you went there. One boy was captured at Cinco Castillos. The other was captured by the Jicarillas up north and traded to the Mescaleros. Which of those two boys did you ransom?"

"I can't remember."

"Where is the boy you ransomed?"

"I never saw him again."

"The woman who had the boy ransomed? Her name was Rafaela Diaz, was it not?"

"I knew her only as Señora Luz. Today she is known as Doña Luz."

"Where is she?"

The padre was surprised. "Surely you know who she is?"

"I would not have asked had I known," said Lee patiently. "Does she live in Santa Fe?"

"She has a great fine house on the Taos Road. She does not have a good reputation, my son."

"Why?"

"When she came here, she asked me to ransom her son. She had no money. She was very young and beautiful. She had no skills. It took many months for her to get the money to buy trade goods to ransom the boy. She had

102

sold the only asset she had—her body. She became a whore, my son. In time, she became what you Anglos call a madam, with many girls working for her. Today she has an establishment for drinking, gambling, and prostitution. She is said to be very wealthy."

Lee shook his head. "Mother of God," he said quietly.

"If you seek her son, I warn you that she would do anything to protect him. She can be a very dangerous woman when crossed."

"Her son is still alive then?"

The padre shrugged. "So it is said. I do not know."

"Will you take care of this little one for me for a few hours? My horse is outside. I took the liberty of putting him in the stable behind the chapel."

The padre nodded. "The boy will be fed and given a place to sleep, my son."

"I won't be gone that long."

Lee walked toward the door. Once he looked back. The padre was again kneeling in prayer with little Basilio Melgosa kneeling beside him with bowed head, aping the old priest. Lee softly closed the door behind himself.

Lee walked into the establishment of Doña

Luz. It was as the padre had said—for drinking, gambling, and prostitution. He stood at the long bar and drank good brandy. He watched a dark-haired beauty, perhaps in her middle thirties, walking between the tables. An exquisite tortoise shell comb was in her raven hair. Her velvet dress was low on her naked shoulders, and the soft lamplight brought out the ivory tone of her skin.

Doña Luz came along behind the bar. She was truly beautiful, with the great, dark, and almost tragic eyes of the *genizaro* and a complexion like the palest of ivory. Diamond earrings flashed in the light of the many crystal chandeliers. Rings sparkled on her lovely, tapered fingers as she gestured, speaking to her many customers. When she was still, she seemed like a painting done full length in oils by one of the great masters.

It was half past eleven. Lee had found out that she always left the establishment at precisely midnight every night in the week. Lee paid his tab and walked outside into the narrow dark street. A carriage was waiting beside the door of the establishment. Lee looked up at the driver. "Are you for hire?" he asked a little drunkenly.

"No, señor," replied the driver. "I drive only for the Doña Luz."

Lee nodded. He crossed the street and stood in a deep doorway. Minutes ticked past. The driver got down from the box and went inside the establishment.

The door was opened allowing a flood of soft light into the dark street. It reflected from the dark, polished surfaces of the fine carriage. The carriage door waas opened and Doña Luz was helped inside. The door was closed. The carriage moved as the driver climbed to his box. He touched up the matched team of blacks with his whip and drove toward the Taos Road.

The woman looked at the shadowy figure seated on the front seat of the carriage. "If you are drunk, señor," she said, "I will have the carriage stopped, and you may get out. But do not let me see your face, for I will remember it."

"I am not drunk," said Lee in Spanish. "I have come a long way from the south to talk to you about your son."

A street lamp flicked its light into the carriage window and against the lovely face of the woman. "I have no son," said Doña Luz.

A big hand was held over toward her. In it

rested a curiously embossed silver button. Another hand came out, holding the opened photograph case. She glanced at the contents of the hands and then looked toward the shadowed face. "Where did you get these?" she asked.

"Duke Bowman, señora," replied Lee.

"What do you want of my son?"

"His father wants to see him."

"I have no son," she said.

"His name was Bart. You took him from the Broken Bow eighteen years ago. He was taken by the Mescaleros at Cinco Castillos. You did not die in the massacre, señora. The grave once marked with the name of Rafaela Diaz holds only mule bones. A man by the name of Candelario Melgosa, a *Penitente*, took you north with him to his village near Las Trampas. You did not stay there long. You came here to raise money to buy trade goods to ransom your son. You sent a priest by the name of Padre Nicolás to deal with the Mescaleros. He brought back a small boy. He would be a man grown now. Where is he?"

"You know much," said the woman. "Perhaps you know *too* much."

"I was warned that you would do anything

106

to protect your son and that you can be a dangerous woman when crossed."

She laughed. "All women are dangerous when crossed, señor."

The carriage was beyond the last of the houses of Santa Fe proper. Lee looked out of the carriage window. There was no sign of anyone else on the road.

"Are you afraid of being followed?" she asked.

"Not afraid, señora, just cautious."

"You may be one of the few living persons who knows my true name and origin," she said.

"Your secret is safe with me," responded Lee.

"As long as I do what you say. How much is Duke paying you to find my son?"

"A thousand a week," replied Lee.

The carriage rolled to a halt. The driver shouted. The wide *zaguán* doors of a high walled house were opened, and the carriage was driven within. The doors were slammed shut behind the carriage, and a heavy wooden bar was dropped into place. The woman smiled at Lee. "Safe at home," she said. Her dark eyes were enigmatic.

The driver opened the door, and his eyes

went wide with astonishment when he saw Lee descend after Doña Luz. He opened and then closed his mouth. He knew better than to question any of her activities, and strange men often came to the great house on the Taos Road. Lee looked beyond the driver. Two men stood just within the doorway watching him. He followed Doña Luz into her living room and closed the door behind himself.

Flickering firelight reflected from the highly polished surface of a grand piano. It shone dully on massive silver candlesticks in which slender candles burned. The candlelight shone on the full-length portrait in oils that hung over the fireplace. It was a twin in dress to the woman who now stand taking off her filmy *rebozo* while she looked into the fire.

"What do you see in the color painting of the embers, Doña Luz?" asked Lee. It was the same question he had asked Duke Bowman not so long past.

"I'll give you five thousand dollars in cash to walk out of here tonight and to forget that you ever saw me."

"I have been contracted to find Bart."

She raised her eyebrows a little. "You have a contract?"

"Verbally, señora."

"And you always hold to them?"

"I have built my reputation on that."

"And you always succeed?"

"I have never failed," he countered.

"I know that is not conceit."

"Professional pride, señora."

She sat down in a chair and looked up at him, studying the lean, bronzed face, the proud nose, the wide gray eyes, and the strong mouth and chin, graced with the short reddish beard. "There is brandy," she suggested.

He filled the glasses. He shaped a cigarette and placed it between her full lips. He lit the cigarette. "I'll double my offer," she said. "Ten thousand dollars."

"Evidently you don't understand," he said as he rolled a cigarette for himself. "I gave my word to Duke Bowman."

"You must think highly of him."

He shook his head. "On the contrary, but business is business."

"And you've risked your life walking in here for a thousand dollars a week?"

Lee shrugged as he lit up. "Professional hazard."

"There is more to it than that," she said

wisely. "You are a man who must live on the very brink of danger. All else is dull and humdrum to you."

"My mother always said I wasn't too bright."

"Twenty thousand," she said. "That's my top offer."

"No alternatives?" he asked as he sat down.

"Only one." She looked at him steadily. "The only people that know you came here tonight are my servants."

"And they won't talk."

"You catch on very quickly."

A subtle transfiguration seemed to have taken place on her beautiful oval face as though it had come from deep within her. It was as though the compound of Spanish and Indian blood had split apart into its separate components, and now she seemed to be pure Indio looking at Lee through her great black eyes.

"Your son would gain much by going back to the Broken Bow with me," argued Lee.

"I can give him almost as much."

"It is his right."

"After eighteen years!" she cried with scorn. "Why now? For all those years, he never once concerned himself about his son or me. Why now?"

110

"His conscience may be bothering him."

"No," she said with conviction. "There is more to it than that. You may as well tell me the full truth."

There was someone close by, thought Lee. Probably behind any, or all, of the three doors that opened into the room. "You know the Dakins," he said.

"The faithful and devout," she sneered.

"No longer, señora. The old man is failing. Marsh Dakin installed his sister, Stella, as Bowman's housekeeper. I think you can guess the rest."

"The old ram couldn't resist getting into bed with her. So now she's probably claiming that she should inherit the Broken Bow because she is his common-law wife."

"She may be able to make it stick," said Lee.

"So now Duke is fighting back the only way he can—by trying to resurrect his long-lost bastard son to take his place. So help me God! Not because he loves the boy as his son, but because he cannot bear to see anyone take over the Broken Bow! Further, I am not such a fool as not to know that the Dakins would do anything to stop you from bringing Bart, *if* he still lives, back to the Broken Bow. I know those people! Marsh Dakin abandoned my son and me at Cinco Castillos."

Lee had no argument about that.

"They thought we both died there," continued Doña Luz. "That was where they made their great mistake. They should have made sure of me."

"But you never had any intention of returning to the Broken Bow," intimated Lee.

"I had learned to hate that old man."

"Because he would not marry you."

She looked into the fire. "I was thinking only of the boy."

Lee laughed. "You wanted that ring of legality on your finger—the circlet of respectability, and a name for your son. Why? Because you are a mixed blood. A *genizaro*! *And so was the boy.* No matter how much Anglo blood the old man had pumped into him, the boy still had the so-called taint of mixed blood, and he always will, and you can't do a damned thing about it!"

She turned her head slowly. There was pure black hate in her great eyes. "I know why you said that. To make my pride force me to tell you where my son is. You've failed."

"What difference can it possibly make now?"

argued Lee. "The Broken Bow can be his. He can be a man in his own right, not waiting on his monthly payment from his mother. Money from a woman he possibly may not know, or what she is either."

"You have much insight," she admitted.

"He knows how you earned the money to pay for his ransom?"

"If you found him, would you tell him?"

"Not if you tell me where he is. I can find him if he is alive, with or without your help. If you don't tell me where he is, I can pay you off in dirty coin by telling him about you and your establishment."

"You wouldn't do that!"

"Try me, señora."

She stood up and reached for a tapestry bell pull.

"Wait," said Lee quietly.

She turned and looked down at the knife in his hand. "You'd never get out of this house alive," she warned.

"I can damned well try. Please walk ahead of me." He opened the door that led into the shadowed patio. A man moved in the shadows. "Tell him to stay where he is," ordered Lee. She held out a warning hand to the man. "Walk into the *sala*," said Lee. She walked to the *sala* door and opened it. A lamp guttered in the hall. The *zaguán* door showed with the great bar across it.

The woman whirled, thrusting her right hand inside the bosom of her dress. Lee thrust his left hand in after her hand and felt the soft, full warmth of her breasts and also the metal and wood of a derringer warmed by her flesh. "I should have known," he said. He pulled out the derringer and dropped it into a pocket. He looked down into her beautiful oval face and drew her close against his hard body, pressed his dry, sun-cracked lips against the soft, moist velvet of her lips.

He heard the soft step behind him. He shoved the woman aside and whirled to drive out a left jab that caught the man on the jaw and dropped him to the floor. His pistol clattered on the tiles. Two more men rushed into the *sala*. Lee thrust the woman between himself and the two men. She snatched up the dropped pistol. He flipped up the door bar and kicked open one of the doors. He ran out into the darkened road.

The rifle flashed from the shadowed brush across the road. Something slapped Lee alongside the head, and as he went down, he caught a second's glimpse of the woman firing across the road into the gunsmoke wreathing through the brush. His face struck the hard road, and he knew no more.

Boots thudded in the brush.

"Let him run," said the woman. She looked down at Lee. "Is he dead?"

One of the men knelt beside Lee. "He's alive," he reported. "He's just been creased. Half an inch more, and he would have been killed."

"Ramón, you and Jesus get him into the house. José, kick dust over that blood on the road and then come with me." She walked toward the far side of the road. A huddled figure lay in the brush. José lighted a match. They looked down into the dark face of Nuno Mercado. A blackened hole in the center of his forehead oozed blood and matter. José looked at her in admiration. "Bull's eye," he said.

She shrugged. "Get rid of this carrion tonight. Don't leave any traces." She walked back to the house.

Somewhere in the darkened hills a coyote howled.

13

THE aura was subtle, yet insistent—a skillful blend of expensive perfume, delicate odor of wax candles, fresh linen, and the feminine scent, half compelling and half repelling. The hard hand cupped itself under Lee's jaw and raised his head, turning it a little to one side. "He'll live," the man said in Spanish. "I've seen wild horses creased like this for the capturing. They were all right later."

"Creasing will not tame this one," the woman said drily.

"Such men do not die easily," said the man.

Lee opened his eyes. He looked up into the lean, bearded face of the man named Ramón. "Looking at you, I'm damned sure I'm not in Heaven," he said.

"I told you, Ramón," said the woman.

Lee looked at her. "You shoot fast," he remarked. "Did you score, Doña Luz?"

She did not reply, but he could read the answer in her face.

"Who died out there in the brush?" he asked.

"A New Mexican. Dark of skin. Pock-marked. Heavy mustache. There was a scar on his forehead. The other man was nothing but a shadow in the darkness as he ran."

She jerked her head toward the door, and Ramón left the room. The opened door revealed that it was full daylight outside. She smoothed the coverlet with her graceful, tapered hands. "No one, outside of me and my people, *and* the man who ran off, knows that you are here. Some of my people are in town now looking about for him."

"So, you are keeping me here to save my life?"

She filled a glass with brandy and held it out to him. "You could say that, although that is not the only reason."

He took the brandy glass and looked into her enigmatic eyes. "You could have gotten rid of me, and no one would have been the wiser."

"I still think I can convince you of the futility of looking for my son. My offer of twenty thousand dollars still stands."

Lee sipped the brandy. "I have a contract," he replied.

She walked to the door and looked back. "Your life is in my hands, señor. Think it over.

You'd be a fool to try and escape, and even if you did, those who tried to kill you will certainly try again. They almost killed you last night. Think that over." She closed the door behind her.

Lee was out of bed at once. He took two steps, swayed sideways, clutched at the table, upset a silver candlestick, and crashed to the floor alongside it. The door was opened. Ramón and another man came in and lifted Lee into the bed. Ramón pulled the coverlet up about Lee. There was a dark bruise on the side of the New Mexican's face, and Lee had an uncomfortable feeling that he was the man that Lee had dropped to the tiles.

"Is there anything you want?" aked Ramón.

Lee grinned. "My pants and a gun," he replied.

Ramón walked to the door. He looked back once as he followed the other man from the room. "The next time you try to get out of here we won't be so gentle." He closed the door behind himself. The lock clicked as the key was turned from the outside.

The boy Basilio was still with Padre Nicolás. If Doña Luz found out about him, she might very well take the boy from the old priest and use him to pressure Lee into abandoning his hunt for her son.

"The boy means nothing to you," the mind voice said. "What is he after all? Just a pawn in this dangerous game."

Lee reached over and refilled his brandy glass.

"Take the twenty thousand *and* the woman," suggested the mind voice.

Lee sipped the powerful brandy. He closed his eyes. The beautiful oval face of Doña Luz, studying him thoughtfully, seemed to come through the mists of pain in his aching skull.

Once during that night, the door to the next room softly opened shortly after Lee had called out in pain. The woman came to the side of the bed. She wore a sheer negligee, and her long, dark hair was unbound about her bare shoulders. She placed a soft cool hand on Lee's fevered brow. At the time, he thought it was a dream.

14

"YOU should have made sure of him," said Stella Dakin. She still wore her traveling costume, an outmoded basque coat and a ridiculous hat that sat atop her head supporting a slightly dusty stuffed bird with staring glass eyes.

Cass sat on the hotel bed with his back against the brass headstead and his booted feet planted on the cover. "If it wasn't for that damned woman, we would have had him cold," he complained.

Reata lighted a cigar. He tilted his chair back against the wall. "Who is this woman?" he asked around the cigar.

"Doña Luz," replied Cass. "She runs a combination saloon, gambling hall, and whorehouse. We saw Kershaw riding in her carriage out to her big *casa* on the Taos Road. We waited in the brush across the road, like I said. Kershaw came bustin' through the door in one helluva hurry. I got in one shot and dropped him, but the woman fired and dropped Nuno.

When I came back, I couldn't find Nuno's body. Kershaw's body was gone too."

"You should have stayed and shot it out!" snapped Stella.

"There was three men come outa that *casa*!" yelled back Cass. "You think I wanted to get shot to doll rags?"

"It would have been all right with me," she said coldly. "You've made a botch out of this, Cass. Both Chisos and Nuno are dead, and Kershaw is still loose."

"He's dead!" yelled Cass. "I don't miss with the long gun."

"You don't know for sure," said Reata.

"What happened to the cholo kid he brought here to Santa Fe?" asked Stella.

"While I was waitin' for you and Reata to get here, I poked about the town asking a few questions. When Kershaw reached here, he took the kid to a chapel out near the hills and left the kid with an old padre out there —name of Padre Nicolás. The kid is still there."

"Go get him," ordered Stella.

"Why?"

Stella took off her hat. "Because we might be able to use him to get to Kershaw, if Kershaw

121

is still alive. Reata, you'd better go along so Cass can't botch this deal up, like he's done everything else."

Reata dropped his chair to the floor and stood up. "Should we bring the kid here?"

She nodded as she took off her coat. "I'm going to get some sleep. That damned train ride wore me out."

Reata closed the door behind himself. He looked at Cass. "Jesus, but she's riled. She's been that way ever since she got the telegram from you. She chewed out Sid for not going along with you like Marsh told him to."

"Sid is too goddamned lazy," said Cass.

"Maybe so, but he'd have never let Kershaw get this far."

They walked together to the stairs. "I still can't believe Kershaw beat Chisos to the draw," said Reata.

"He never done it! He tricked Chisos. He don't fight fair!"

Reata looked sideways at the stupid face of the big man. "Why should he in this business? It's the results that count. So, Chisos is dead, and if Kershaw is dead like you claim he is, you didn't exactly give him a fair shake by drygulching him."

"That's different!" snapped Cass.

Reata shook his head as he walked down the stairs and into the lobby. "Cass," he said quietly, "sometimes I can't believe you."

They stopped outside the hotel while Cass rolled a cigarette. Cass lit the quirly. "Nuno claimed he knew one of us would not return from the north," he said quietly.

"So? It's him that's dead, ain't it?"

Cass nodded. He looked across the plaza as though seeking something in the shadows on the far side of it. "He always claimed Kershaw wasn't human. He said he could do things no other living man could do."

Reata grinned around his cigar.

It was as though Cass was talking to himself. "He crossed the waterless desert northeast from Tinaja del Muerto in the furnace heat to reach North Pass. He got into the Broken Bow without being seen by any of us, and he got out the same way. He reached Cinco Castillos and got away right under our noses. He went into them mountains full of Mescaleros and came out alive. He killed Chisos Martin, the fastest man with a cutter I've ever seen.

He got drinkin' water out of a salt *laguna* —something I don't think Moses himself coulda done by striking the ground with his staff. He got north to Santa Fe without us catching him, and we rode two horses to death."

"Luck," said Reata.

Cass shook his head.

"What makes you think it ain't?"

"Reata, you know I'm as good a man with the long gun as you've ever seen. I couldn't have missed him the other night. It wasn't possible. I *know* I put a bullet into his *cabeza*."

"I believe you, Cass."

"Only one thing," said Cass slowly. "Supposin' he was taken into that woman's *casa* on the Taos Road? Supposin' he's still walkin' around?"

"Well he is, or he ain't." Reata looked quickly at Cass as he caught the full meaning of what the big man had said. "For Christ's sake!" he rapped out. "You're talkin' like a superstitious cholo now! He's either dead, or he ain't; and if he is, he ain't doin' any walkin' around! Not on this earth, he ain't! Now come on! I'll buy the liquor. We can get the kid later."

Jesus stepped out of a doorway beside the hotel as Reata and Cass walked toward a sloon. "It's him, Les," he said over his shoulder. "That's the big man who shot at Kershaw night before last. The other one is the man who came up from the train at Lamy on the stagecoach along with the woman who wears the dead bird on her head."

"Who's the kid they were talking about?"

Jesus shrugged. "I know old Padre Nicolás," he said. "He takes care of a little chapel out near the hills. No one ever goes in there anymore. While they're drinking, you've just got time to get back to Doña Luz and ask her what we should do. I'll keep an eye on those two men. I need a drink or two myself." He grinned.

Les mounted his horse and rode off down a side street. Jesus fashioned a cigarette and walked into the hotel lobby. "I'm looking for a woman who registered here tonight," he said to the desk clerk.

"Only one woman registered here tonight," said the clerk. He turned the register. "See here? Stella Dakin, Running MB."

"That isn't her. Where is the Running MB?"

The clerk shrugged. "Broken Bow country, I think. Down south of the Rio Penasco and west of the Pecos."

Jesus walked outside and headed for the saloon.

Reata softly opened the chapel door. The warm candle-scented air blew about him and Cass. The slight bowed figure of the padre knelt before the altar. There was a much smaller figure beside the padre, aping his posture of bowed head and clasped hands. There was no one else in the chapel.

The two Anglos walked softly up the nave aisle. The soft, flickering candlelight reflected from the great reredos behind the altar and from the flesh and blood tones of the agonized Christ on his cross.

Basilio slowly turned his head and looked up into the two hard faces shadowed under the wide hat brims. "This is the house of God, señores," he piped. "We are at prayer."

"Get up, kid," said Reata. "We're going to take you to your mother."

"I have no mother, señor."

Reata yanked the kid to his feet. He jerked

126

his head toward the padre. "Start asking your questions, Cass," he said.

Cass reached out with a huge hand and touched the shoulder of Padre Nicolás. The old man fell slowly sideways and lay still. Cass knelt and looked into the waxlike face. "He's dead," he said over his shoulder.

The footsteps of Reata and Basilio echoed in the empty chapel. The door closed behind them.

Cass stood up and looked down at the dead priest. He could not take his eyes from the composed and peaceful face of the old man. It was deathly quiet in the chapel. The candle flames stood straight up in the draftless air. The light of the candles reflected from the staring eyes of the old priest, and they were looking directly up at Cass Dakin. The memory of another old man who had died under his fist came back to Cass. He too had stared up at Cass in the same accusing way. Cass looked quickly at the agonized face of the Christ. The carved eyes seemed to be staring at him too.

Suddenly there seemed to be a faint murmuring of accusing voices in the shadowed corners of the chapel and in the dark choir loft. Cass turned on a heel and ran from the chapel.

He slammed the door behind him and fell over a body lying across the steps. He was half stunned. He sat up and wiped the blood from his face. He lighted a match and looked into the pale face of Reata. Reata's hat had fallen off and a large lump, tinged with blood showed on the side of his head. He was still alive.

Cass got to his feet and looked quickly about. "Kid?" he called out. There was no answer. The narrow street was deserted.

15

LEE heard the *zaguán* door slam shut, followed by the rattling of hoofs and the grinding of wheels on the tiles. The door bar was dropped into place. He heard the faint murmuring of voices. Footsteps sounded outside, and the door was unlocked. Doña Luz walked in, removing her robozo from over her fine tortoiseshell comb and dark hair.

Lee filled two wineglasses. "You're late tonight," he said.

She nodded. "There was some business to attend to." She sat down in the chair opposite to his. He made a cigarette and reached over to place it between her full lips. He lit it for her as she bent forward, and he had a hard time keeping his eyes on hers with the daring decolletage she affected. He leaned back and shaped a cigarette for himself. "Damned if I'm not beginning to like it here, Doña Luz," he said.

"There are some people who have come here from the south. A man and a woman. They met

129

with the man who managed to escape the other night. She is Stella Dakin. He is know as Reata. I did not know either of them in my time at the Broken Bow."

"They are bringing in the first-line troops," he said.

"A woman?" she asked, arching her eyebrows.

"The deadly species," he said. "Do you suppose they know who you really are?"

She shrugged. "I doubt it." She smiled a little. "You are probably the only person here in Santa Fe who knows who I really am."

"You forget Padre Nicolás."

"He died this evening," she said.

"Suddenly I feel very alone."

"Your friends from the south are not sure that you are alive. In fact, the only people that *do* know you are alive are myself and my servants."

Lee inspected his cigarette as though he had never seen one before. "It's not a very comforting thought."

"Have you reconsidered my offer?"

"I have. The answer is the same."

"You could agree and take the twenty thousand and continue hunting for my son, could you not?"

"I don't do business that way." He refilled her wineglass. "You must think I am a fool."

She shook her head. "Obstinate, but not a fool. You haven't asked me about the small boy Basilio you left with Padre Nicolás."

Lee studied her. "What about him?" he asked.

She walked to the door and opened it. "Send in the boy!" she called out. The sober little face of Basilio Melgosa appeared in the doorway. She closed the door behind him and watched him run to Lee with outstretched arms. Lee gathered up the small figure.

"Very touching," she drily commented.

"Are you all right, *muchacho*?" he asked.

"I am fine," replied Basilio.

Lee looked over Basilio's dark head at the woman. "You play dirty," he said.

"Bart was about that age and size when we reached Cinco Castillos," she said quietly. Her great eyes studied Lee. "Can you see now why I did what I had to do to get him back?"

"But you didn't really get him back at all."

There was sudden deep pain within her eyes.

131

She looked quickly away from him. "At least he did not go back to his father," she said.

"So now neither one of you has him."

"It is enough for me that his father does not have him!" she cried.

"How did you find the boy?"

"Those people went to the chapel to get him. I was told they were going there. I didn't know who the boy was. My men took him away from them and brought him here."

"What happens now to the boy?"

She smiled confidently. "*That,* is up to *you.*"

"You seem to hold all the aces."

"I am a professional," she countered.

"Has it ever occurred to you that Duke Bowman is a dying man and that if Bart does not go there to take his rightful inheritance, it will likely pass into the hands of the Dakins?"

"The place means nothing to me! I hated it when I was there, and I hate it now!"

He studied her. "That's not true. How many years do you think you can get away with sending money to your son, wherever he is, without him trying to find out who you really are? He's a grown man now, not a boy. He can't go on through life like that. He has to

132

make his own way. What better way than for him to take his place at the Broken Bow? In time, he could send for you, Doña Luz."

"Never!"

Lee shrugged. "I still intend to find him."

"Have you forgotten that I hold all the aces?"

He studied her. "If you intended to kill me, Doña Luz, you would never have allowed me to regain consciousness, nor stay here alive in this fine *casa* of yours."

She threw her cigarette into the fireplace. "Make me another," she said. She watched his skilful fingers mold the cigarette. "I've kept you alive because I think it might be interesting to tame you."

He placed the cigarette between her lips. "That can work both ways between a woman like yourself and a man like me." Take the twenty thousand, *and* the woman—the thought coursed through his mind.

"I could use a man like you in my business," she suggested.

"As a partner?"

"Hardly. Perhaps after a time."

"So you'd use me as a bartender, a stool pigeon, a shill, or a bouncer? Or perhaps as a pimp?"

She laughed delightedly. "No! But, we'd make a good team, Lee Kershaw. I don't like to admit it, but I need a *man*."

"Santa Fe is full of men."

"None like you."

"I want to go home," said Basilio.

She looked down at him. He smiled winningly at her.

"And what about him?" asked Lee.

"We can send him home," Doña Luz suggested. "Where does he live?"

"A small village near Las Trampas. His people are *Penitentes*. His great-uncle is *Hermano Mayor* there."

Her eyes narrowed. "Sostenes Melgosa?"

Lee nodded. "You knew that village. Candelario Melgosa took you there after Cinco Castillos."

"I was only there a little while."

"There are *genizaros* there, Doña Luz."

"My people are from the *Valle de Lagrimas*."

Lee shook his head. "Your people are of the north. Perhaps from the very village where Basilio lived."

She walked to the door. "Jesus!" she called out as she opened it. "Come and get the boy.

Feed him and put him to bed. Do not let him get out of this house. You understand?"

She closed the door after Jesus came for the boy. She looked at Lee. "Do you always know too much about people?"

"It is my business."

"A dangerous business."

He shrugged. "I get paid well," he counterd.

"You have until tomorrow to accept my final offer."

He looked up at her. "You're very tired," he suggested. "How long can you keep on in the role of Doña Luz, Rafaela Diaz?"

"Tomorrow is Sunday," she said quietly. "A day of rest for me and a day of decision for you. The wise man takes the bird in hand." She waved a hand toward the door. "Out there is death for you. Here there is security."

"And domination by a woman," added Lee drily.

He refilled her glass. "I thought I had a dream the other night," he said. "There was a fever in me, and I cried out in pain. A woman came to me in the darkness and cooled my fever with a healing hand." He looked into her dark eyes. "But it must have been a dream."

She drained her glass and walked to the door

that opened into her room. "Good night, señor. Always remember that it is easy for me to hear you cry out in here." She closed the door behind herself. The key did not click in the lock.

Lee blew out the candles and sat in the chair for a long time looking into the shifting, weaving kaleidoscope of color in the embers of the fireplace.

The clock struck half past one. Lee emptied his wineglass and threw his cigarette butt into the embers. He walked to the bed and called out as though caught again in the fever. He lay down on the wide bed.

The door softly opened. She came quickly and silently across the room to place a cool hand on his forehead. Her long dark hair brushed his chests and face. He drew her down to him and pressed his mouth hard against hers. She did not struggle. "The fever seems to have left," she murmured as he withdrew his lips from hers.

"It's not the same one," he said. "Can you cure the other one?" She placed her cools hands on each side of his face.

"Remember that you are my prisoner," she

reminded him, "and that I am responsible for your health."

She was a woman who had known many different men in her lifetime since the age of fifteen when Duke Bowman had bulled her, as he called it. Now Lee found out how she had been so successful in her earlier profession. She gave Lee the impression that he was the only one who had been able to satisfy her, and yet he wasn't even sure that was so. He'd never admit it to her, but he had never known a woman quite like Rafaela Diaz.

She lay quietly beside him, resting her head against his shoulder with the faint glowing of her cigarette tip alternately lighting and shadowing her oval face. The soft light glistened from the beads of perspiration on her full breasts. "You will take my offer then?" she asked.

He nodded. "Of course. But you can keep the twenty thousand."

She laughed. "How generous! But then, by staying with me, you'll stand to gain a great deal more than that cold money, my heart."

He passed a hand over her full body. "I've got the general idea," he admitted.

The clock struck half past two.

"Bart lives in the same small village where I sent him years ago," she said suddenly. "The one near Las Trampas, which Basilio calls his home."

"Why tell me now?"

She shrugged. "You'll find out soon enough. He lives with an uncle of mine, Gaspar Diaz. He is called Innocencio Diaz. He has been raised as a *Penitente*."

"Then thank God he does not know how his mother lives."

"He never will," she said.

He got up and refilled the wineglasses. He looked down at her. Candelario Melgosa had not mentioned Bart living in his village, but then maybe the old man had been sworn to secrecy by Rafaela Diaz. He held the glass to her full lips, and she drank greedily. He downed his wine and sat down on the edge of the bed, passing his strong hard hands up and down her body.

"So soon again, my heart?" she murmured.

"Look at me, my life," he said. She turned her lovely face toward him. His right cross caught her jaw at exactly the right angle. She lay still.

Lee stood up. He took a drink straight from

the decanter and looked down at her body in the dimness. "*Madre mia*," he breathed regretfully. He tied her ankles and wrists together with strips of her negligee and then gagged her.

He walked into the room in which she had slept while he had occupied her room. His clothing was in a wardrobe. His Colt was in a locked drawer which he had to pry open. He felt within his pockets and found the silver button and the photograph. Even his tobacco makings were in a pocket. He checked the Colt to find it loaded.

Lee rummaged through a desk. He found an address book which he slipped into a pocket. He could not find any letters. He eased open the outer door and looked into the dark patio. It seemed empty of life.

He found Basilio sound asleep in a small room. He placed a hand over the boy's mouth to awaken him. "*Muchacho*," he whispered. "We play a game, eh? Do not make a sound."

The boy shook his head. "I don't like it here," he whispered.

"Neither do I," agreed Lee. He carried Basilio from the room.

A tiny spot of flame arced out into the center of the patio and exploded into a shower of sparks as the cigarette butt struck the tiles. Lee faded into the deep shadows. Footsteps sounded near the entrance to the *sala*.

Lee climbed to the flat roof and carried the boy across it. He hung by one arm from the parapeted roof and dropped lightly into the shrubbery.

Reata raised his head from the shelter of the brush across the road from the great *casa* of Doña Luz. Nothing moved. The night was graveyard still under the flickering stars.

The barrel of a Colt was laid hard and true —right across the side of Reata's head just between the top of the right ear and the brim of the hat. Reata went down silently. Boots grated softly on the hard ground in the shadowed brush.

The chapel was dark and still when Lee reached it. He saddled the dun within the stable and withdrew the Winchester from the saddle scabbard to check the loads. He led the dun from the stable. Swiftly he walked inside the dark and empty chapel. He lit a candle for the repose of the soul of Padre Nicolás and then closed the door behind himself. In a little while, hoofbeats sounded on the road that led north toward Las Trampas.

16

THE moonlight was bright on the piñon-dotted hills that sloped away on either side of the narrow road leading into a narrow gutted canyon. There was no wind to move the dark piñons and the thorned brush that encroached on the sides of the road. The only sign of life in the dreamlike landscape was a straight line of smoke, which rose from the chimney of the first of the houses that lined the road in the gut of the canyon.

Lee looked down at Basilio. "Is this your home, boy?"

"Yes—home," said Basilio happily.

Lee shrugged. Any place would be home to Basilio if it pleased Lee.

The country was isolated, remote, far from the better traveled roads north of Santa Fe and south from Taos. It was the home and refuge of *La Hermandad de Nuestro Padre Jesus* and had been so since the sixteenth and seventeeth centuries. The inhabitants were descendents of the first Spanish colonials and even now their daily life and customs were almost the same as those of the sixteenth century Spanish peasants. So was their religion and their brotherhood of *Penitentes*, preserved as though in a dusty museum case.

"He lives with an uncle of mine, Gaspar Diaz. He is called Innocencio Diaz. He has been raised as a *Penitente*," Doña Luz had told Lee.

"I want to go home," said Basilio.

He too was of *Penitente* blood, the great-grandson of Candelario Melgosa, the *Enfermero* of the Brotherhood, and the great-nephew of Sostenes Melgosa, the *Hermano Mayor*—the highest elected official of the Brotherhood.

"*Largate! Largate!*" the mind voice warned Lee. "Go away."

The hoofs of the dun clattered on the sharp-edged stones, or *pedernales* of the road and awoke the sleeping echoes in the dreamlike hills. There was a windowless, coffin-shaped building on a knoll to the left, just before the first houses of the village. At the tip of the steeply pitched roof of the *morada*, the white-washed cross shone in the moonlight as though fashioned of long-bleached bones. In front of the *morada*, there was another whitewashed cross with laths placed on either side from the tip of the upright to the tips of the arms, and with other laths placed from the tips of the arms down to the sides of the upright. It formed a square set on one point and quartered by the upright and crosspiece. Placed within the four equilateral triangles formed by the laths and the parts of the cross were other, smaller crosses, two to each triangle; and on the upper slanting parts of the diagonal laths, there were similar crosses. Lying on the barren ground in front of this ornate cross were other crosses, fashioned of immensely heavy beams; these were carried by penitent brothers during the Holy Week rites of the Brotherhood.

"*Largate!*" a harsh voice suddenly called out.

Lee reined in the dun. A man walked from the thick brush into the center of the road in front of Lee. He held a rifle in his brown hands. "*Largate!*" he repeated.

Something made Lee turn his head. The road was filled from side to side and five men deep with other villagers. Some of them reached down to pick up the murderous, razor-edged flint stones, the *pedernales*. These were the stones used by the *Penitente Sangrador*, or *Picador*, the Blood Letter or Pricker, to inflict the seal of the Brotherhood—three horizontal and three vertical gashes across the naked backs of the novices of the *Hermanos de Sangre*, or Brothers of Blood.

The first stone struck the back of Lee's left hand and instantly drew forth the bright blood. "Wait!" yelled Lee. He held up the boy. "I have brought the boy Basilio Melgosa home to his great-uncle, the *Hermano Mayor* Sostenes Melgosa!" Before God, thought Lee, suppose, just suppose now that this was *not* the village of the Melgosas.

"Wait here," ordered the sentry. He walked to the first house on the right-hand side of the street. An old man came to the door and then walked slowly up the center of the road toward Lee.

Lee glanced back at the silent watching figures. They could batter him to death in minutes if they wished. No one in the outside world would be any the wiser if they did so. His body would never be found. If anyone came looking for him, they would learn nothing. These people were a world apart from nineteenth century New Mexico Territory; a closed society for over three hundred years.

The man was old. His hair under the sides

of his ancient felt sombrero was as white as the snow-capped tips of the neighboring Sangre de Cristo Mountains in the winter time. "Who asks for Sostenes Melgosa?" he asked.

"I do," replied Lee. "I have brought home Basilio Melgosa."

"Where is his great-grandfather, my brother, Candelario?"

"He is dead, señor," replied Lee. He held up the boy. "See? Here is little Basilio."

The old man raised his head. The moonlight fell upon his dried apple of a face; his eyes were like pools of milk.

"Christ's blood!" said Lee in a low voice. He slewed his eyes sideways wondering how far he'd make it off the road into the thorned brush before a murderous flight of *pedernales* brought him down.

"Send the boy to me, señor," said the blind old man.

Lee let the boy down onto the road. He ran with outstretched arms to the old man. The man spoke softly to the boy and then looked over Basilio's head toward Lee. "You are welcome here, señor," he said. "My house is your house."

146

Lee passed his bloody left hand across his eyes. "*Mil gracias*," he said.

"You know of the Brotherhood, I think," said Sostenes.

Lee glanced back over his shoulder. The road was empty. "Some," admitted Lee.

"You happened to come here at a time when strangers are not welcome."

"It was not intentional, *Hermano Mayor*. I came here to bring back the boy, not to stare at your rites. Your beliefs are your own. I honor them as I know you would mine."

The old man bowed his head. "You do not have to leave tonight. There is room for you and the boy in my house this night. But it would be better if you left by daylight tomorrow."

Lee dismounted and led the tired dun toward the old man. Together he, Basilio, and Sostenes walked toward the house. "There is another reason you have come here?" questioned Sostenes.

"I am looking for a man. But I would have brought the boy back in any case. It is a coincidence that the man lives here in your village. His name is Innocencio Diaz."

"You are a man of the law?"

147

"No. I was hired to find him for his own good."

"Who hired you?"

"His father."

"That is very strange, for his father is long dead."

"That is not so," said Lee. "But, in any case, his mother said he lived here."

"His mother is also dead."

Lee opened and then closed his mouth. Perhaps Rafaela Diaz wanted it that way. "I'd like to see him," he said.

They stopped in front of the house. "Later I will tell you about him," said Sostenes. The milk-white eyes looked at Lee almost as though the old man could actually see him. "You do not lie to me when you tell me you are not from the law?"

"I am not from the law," repeated Lee.

"There is a corral behind this house. Put your horse there. There is food in the house to which you are welcome. There are *colchones* for your bed. Now, listen to me: Once you go into my house tonight, do not come out of it again. Do not look from the windows or the door, no matter what happens. If you do, I will not be responsible for what happens to you. Do you understand?"

"I understand."

Sostenes nodded. "*Bueno*! And now, good night, señor."

Lee watched the old man walk up the street where the canyon curved away out of sight.

Once again it seemed like a dream world. It was as though Lee Kershaw had been spirited back in time to sixteenth century New Mexico. There was no wind; there was no movement of any kind; there was no sound to break the deathlike quiet of the village and the surrounding hills. The coffin-shaped *morada* squatted in the moonlight. The crosses shone ghastly white like well-polished bones.

Lee unsaddled the tired dun. Now and again, he would look quickly over his shoulder as though he felt someone were watching him, but he never saw anyone. He knew they were out there nevertheless. He went into the little house and lit a lamp. Basilio was sound asleep on the *colchones*, or bed mattresses, spread on the hard-packed dirt floor.

Lee was not hungry. His skull ached where the bullet had creased it. He made a cigarette. Slowly he raised his head. A faint piping sound,

149

almost indistinguishable, seemed to drift down the canyon, and then it died away.

He lit the cigarette. The sound came again, this time accompanied by a strident clacking sound. Lee threw the cigarette into the beehive fireplace. He blew out the lamp. He catfooted to one of the small front windows and eased open one of the shutters until it caught on the loose catch, leaving a gap of perhaps an inch. He peered up the moonlit street of the village toward the bend in the canyon where the shadows met the moonlight on the whitish road in a sharp line of demarcation, black-on-white.

The sound came closer; the thin, reedy piping and the crisp rattling sound of the *matraca*. Piping, in the villages of the Brotherhood, was never done for pleasure, but only during their rites. The sound now echoed from the narrow sides of the canyon.

Sostenes Melgosa appeared in the moonlight, walking in the center of the street and striking the ground at every second step with an ironshod staff. Behind him came a man with bent head, reading prayers, aloud from a copybook. The *Pitero*, or Piper, was next, accompanied by a man plying the *matraca* or clacker. The next man in the procession was bent over, walking deliberately on the razor-edged *pedernales* with his bare feet which left bloody footprints on the moonlit ground. His head was shrouded in a black hood, and he was naked from the waist up, wearing only short white trousers. In his strong brown hands, he held a *disciplina*, a whip of leather thongs embellished with tight knots, shards of glass, and bits of barbed wire. First the *disciplina* was swung over the right shoulder and then the left, in perfect cadence with the measured footsteps of the procession and the rhythm of the pipe and clacker. As the *disciplina* slashed home against the small of the man's naked back, bright droplets of blood flew out on both sides to speckle the ground. Behind the penitent was a man—a *Hermano de Luz*, a Brother of the Light, whose duty was to see that the penitent did not stint in the force of his blows.

"*Yo penitente pecador!*" cried out the penitent.

"I, a repentant sinner," translated Lee to himself.

Two more penitents appeared, accompanied by a *Hermano de Luz*. One of them swung a *disciplina* of barbed chain link, and the other one used one of the stripped fibers of the yucca

151

plant. Each of them drew blood equally well. The glittering droplets of blood spattered in the moonlight. Now and again, one of the penitents would stagger in his stride from the savage force of the blows he was administering to himself. The eerie whistling of the pipe and the monotonous clacking of the *matraca* was in time with the crying of the penitents: *"Yo penitente pecador! Yo penitente pecador! Yo penitente pecador!"*

Six men appeared in the moonlight. A crudely made casket without a top was balanced on their shoulders. Lee could just make out the form within the casket. It was a man of slight build.

The strange and eerie funeral procession walked up the slope to the *morada* and into it. The door slammed shut, and the thick windowless walls cut off any sound from within.

The sudden silence was startling. It was as though there had been a dream procession. But the dark spots of blood flecking the light-colored road were proof enough that a *Penitente* procession had passed.

"Why at night?" said Lee aloud.

Lee smoked a cigarette, watching the *morada*, but no one appeared at the door. He lay down on the *colchones*. The memory of the cry "*Largate!*" coupled with the recollection of the murderous *pedernales*, was enough to keep Lee within doors that moonlit night.

Lee opened his eyes. He got up and walked to the window. The dying moonlight slanted down into the canyon and touched the *morada*. The door gaped opened. No sound came from within. There was no sign of life anywhere near it.

Lee left the house by the back door. He circled through the shadows and approached the *morada* from the rear. He walked on the shadowed side to the front of it. He flattened himself against the front wall and looked back over his shoulder into the dark interior. The waxy odor of candles and lamp oil came to him. He stepped inside quickly and closed the door behind himself. It was pitch black, and it seemed to him that the air within the *morada* was breathing slowly and heavily.

He lit a match. He looked into a miniature skull face, shrouded in a black shawl. It was Doña Sebastiana, the Angel of Death, seated on her heavy wooden cart whose wheels would not turn—the *Carreta de la Muerte*. The cart was usually dragged by several pairs of Brothers by means of horsehair ropes bound about their chests and sometimes around their throats. In her ugly, bony little hands, she held a tiny bow with an arrow nocked to the string, ready to shoot. The light of the match glittered from her deepset eye sockets, and it seemed to Lee that she had a speculative look in them.

He walked to the raised dais at the other end of the *morada* and risked lighting one of the candles. The altar cloth was black and decorated with finely embroidered skulls and crossbones. There were some crude, brightly painted *santos* on the altar, mingled in among several human skulls and a cross mounted on three steps. Lee surveyed the low-ceilinged room. The whitewashed walls were splattered with blood, some long dried, and some still fresh from that very night.

Lee searched about the altar. The Brotherhood kept records of their members, and Lee wanted to know when Innocencio Diaz had been born, and where; and when he had joined the Brotherhood as a *novio* to spend his five years as a penitent, or Brother of Blood, before he could be elevated to a Brother of Light. There were no records to be found within the *morada*.

Lee looked quickly over his shoulder. The candle dimly lit the altar area and the rear of the *morada*. Beyond the flickering pool of soft light were the shadows. Once he thought he saw someone, or *something*, moving stealthily along the blood-splattered wall, and his hand dropped to his Colt. He narrowed his eyes and raised the candle. There was no one there.

Lee blew out the candle and catfooted to the door, resisting an urge to rip open the door and get the hell out of there—*now!*

He eased the door open and slipped around to the shadowed side of the *morada*. He raised his head, thinking he had heard something beyond the ridge. He crossed the moonlit road, got his field glasses, and ghosted through the thorned brush and up the steep side of the ridge, going to ground just below the crest.

Lee focused the glasses on a group of men standing in a cleared area surrounded by the murderous thorned bush. A hole shaped like a grave was in the center of the clearing. The lidless coffin stood beside the grave with the shrouded figure of the dead person plainly visible in the moonlight. As Lee watched, the body was taken from the coffin and the shroud was stripped from it. The fine German lens picked out the emaciated face of a young man, perhaps twenty-five years old. The body was lowered into the grave without the coffin.

One man picked up a heavy rock and slammed it down with his full strength on top of the body. Other mourners did the same, and Lee could plainly hear the heavy thudding of the rocks against the gaunt body. Earth was shoveled back into the grave. Lee looked down the ridge behind himself. The village dreamed in the dying moonlight. There was not a sign of life anywhere within it.

Lee turned to look down at the grave. He narrowed his eyes. The clearing had vanished. The whole area was evenly covered with thorned brush. The Brothers were now walking rapidly toward the ridge. Lee wasted no time. He worked his way swiftly down the treacherous slope and through the ripping, tearing thorns. He looked back from the rear door of Sostenes Melgosa's house. A conical hat was just showing above the ridge. He closed the door behind himself and felt the hot sweat course down his body. He lay down on the *colchones*.

It was very quiet. There was no wind.

Sandals husked in the street. A man coughed. Then it was quiet again.

The front door was opened slowly. Footsteps grated on the dirt floor. A hand was gently placed against Lee's sweating forehead. The hand was lowered and placed over his thudding heart. The hand was withdrawn. Sandals husked on he floor. "He sleeps quietly, my brothers," announced Sostenes Melgosa. "He has not been out of this house. Good night to you all." The door was closed.

"How much did you see?" asked Sostenes from beside the bed.

Lee sat up. "Only a burial," he honestly replied.

"That was too much."

"I came here to find Innocencio Diaz. I haven't much time. I can't find him while lying here on your *colchones*."

"I told you I would tell you about him."

Lee rolled two cigarettes. He placed one between the old man's lips and lit it and his own. "Where is he, *viejo*?" he asked.

"If you saw the burial, you saw Innocencio."

"One of the mourners?"

Sostenes shook his head. "He sleeps," he said.

The thudding of the heavy rocks on the emaciated young body came back to haunt Lee. "He is dead?" asked Lee.

"He sleeps," repeated Sostenes.

"But why all the mystery? Why at night?"

"The Church recently prohibited cross carrying and flagellation in public. We have been condemned for our disregard of the proper authority of the Church. But that is no concern of yours. It merely explains why we conducted a burial this night."

"You explain the reason for performing your rites at night, but you have not explained the secret burial of Innocencio Diaz."

"I am coming to that. You know, of course, that we practice our rites during Holy Week. It is a great honor for one among the Brotherhood to be chosen as the Christo, to be crucified on Good Friday. This year it was Innocencio Diaz who drew the paper pellet with the name Cristo written upon it. A lucky man," Sostenes's voice died away. "I have never been so fortunate," he added after a time.

"Innocencio bore the great cross well. It was a miracle. He was a small man and not very strong, but somehow he managed. He was crucified."

"With nails?" asked Lee incredulously.

"With wet rawhide," replied Sostenes.

Lee looked into the wrinkled face. There was no expression on it.

"The rawhide dries and constricts," continued Sostenes. "The limbs of the Cristo turned blue. His hand fell upon his chest. I, as *Hermano Mayor*, took a blade and made an incision in his side so that the blood gushed forth."

Lee threw his cigarette into the fireplace and quickly shaped another. He placed it between the lips of the old man and lit it. He made another for himself and lit it. "And he died upon the cross, eh, *viejo*?" he asked.

Sostenes shook his head. "Not then, señor. He lived."

"But that was last spring," said Lee.

"He was never the same," explained Sostenes. "If a Brother dies upon the cross enacting the Cristo, his soul is assured of salvation in Heaven. His grave is unmarked and remains secret for one year, and then his relatives are notified. But Innocencio Diaz lived. He could not speak and could hardly walk about. He lasted until yesterday."

"Just my luck," said Lee.

"What does that mean?"

Lee shook his head. "*Nada, nada, viejo*. Go on, please."

The old man shrugged. "We held his wake. The last rites were held in the *morada* tonight. He had requested burial *sin cajon*, without a coffin. We had promised that when he was selected as the Cristo."

Lee nodded. "Well, I hope for his sake, he does have eternal salvation."

"There is no question about that," said Sostenes firmly.

"You say his father and mother are dead?"

"There is no question about that."

'You knew them?"

"Of course. They lived here all their lives."

"He was truly the son of Gaspar Diaz?"

"It is so listed in the book of the Brotherhood."

"I wish I had found that book," said Lee witout thinking.

It was very quiet. The milk-white eyes seemed to fix themselves on Lee's face. "There is a woman, one Rafaela Diaz," quickly put in Lee, "who claims that Innocencio was her son, the union of herself and an Anglo by the name of Mark Bowman, who lives in the south."

"I know that woman," said Sostenes. "Gaspar Diaz was her uncle, and Innocencio was her nephew."

"You are sure of this?"

"My wife was the midwife of this village. The mother of Innocencia had great trouble with his birth. I helped my wife in the delivery. The boy lived; the mother died."

"The lying *puta*," said Lee.

"She too had a son. I saw him once, years ago. She had him taken from this place, and we never saw him again. Have you looked for him in Santa Fe?"

"He's not there," replied Lee.

"One might look in Las Vegas," suggested Sostenes.

"What do you know of him?"

Sostenes shrugged. "Nothing."

Lee knew he would get no more out of the old man.

Sostenes looked steadily at Lee, although he could not see him. "My friend," he said quietly, "there are two reasons why you are still alive, and not dead and buried in an unmarked grave this night. First, you brought my great-nephew Basilio back to me. Second, because I lied to my Brothers by saying that you were asleep and that you had not been out of this house. I am not sure they believed me. Even now they may be talking about you. In any case, I must resign as *Hermano Mayor* and do severe penance because I did lie to them."

Lee had a vivid mind picture of a *disciplina* slashing away at the thin, scarred flesh of the old man's back.

"It would be wise for you to leave here tonight—*now*," warned Sostenes. He raised his head as though to listen. "They may be coming soon."

Lee pulled on his boots. He clapped his hat on his head. He buckled on his gunbelt. "One small favor, *viejo*," he said. "If anyone comes looking for me, you did not see me. You know nothing about me, eh?"

"I owe you that."

Lee looked down at the white head in the darkness. "*Mil gracias*," he said.

"*Por nada*," murmured the old man. His thoughts seemed to be elsewhere. "Go with God, my friend."

The rear door softly closed. In a little while, the sharp ears of the old man picked up the soft sound of rawhided hoofs tapping on the earth beyond the stable. It was very quiet again.

Minutes ticked past. Then the knock Sostenes expected came on the door. He could no longer hear the sound of the hoofsbeats. He opened the door.

17

THE early afternoon sun shone down into the narrow canyon. Sheep drifted over a brown- and salmon-colored ridge, which was dotted with dark piñons looking like cloves stuck in a roasting ham. The faint sound of the *baaing* drifted down the slopes. Bluish smoke wreathed up from the chimneys of the adobes and the *jacals*. A burro brayed harshly from a peeled-pole corral.

Reata reined in his claybank. He narrowed his eyes as he saw the coffin-shaped *morada*, which squatted on the knoll overlooking the one road that ran through the village. Reata turned in his saddle and held up a warning hand to halt the buggy behind them.

Cass Dakin reined in the team. "What's up, Reata?" he called.

Reata rode back to the buggy. "This is a *Penitente* village," he said in a low voice. "See the *morada*?"

"So?" asked Cass.

"They don't talk much to outsiders, especially Anglos."

Stella raised her head impatiently. The dusty bird on her hat bobbed up and down. "You can always *buy* information."

"Not from these people, Stell," said Reata.

"Odds are that Kershaw never came this way, Stell," put in Cass.

"Ask somebody," said Stella.

"Like who?" asked Cass.

"That man in the doorway of that second house," replied Stella.

Cass drove the buggy up the road with his saddle horse trotting along behind it. "You there!" Stella called out peremptorily in cowpen Spanish. "We're looking for a man. Tall, broad in the shoulders, reddish hair and beard. Light gray eyes. A big nose. He had a small boy with him by the name of Basilio Melgosa. Have you seen him?"

The man did not move. His dark eyes studied the two big Anglo men with their hard and cold gringo eyes and their lowslung pistols. The strange woman with the dusty bird on her head seemed even harder and colder than the two men.

"I'm talking to you, mister!" shrilled Stella.

There was no answer from the man. He looked at the road behind the buggy.

Reata slowly turned his head. "Jesus," he said softly.

Cass turned to look. "Now you done it, Stella," he accused.

Stella looked back over her shoulder. A dozen sombreroed men stood in the sunlit road from shoulder to shoulder, so that no horseman or vehicle could pass unless they moved. They had no weapons in their hands. They did not need any. The road and its shoulders were littered with sharp *pedernales*.

Iron clicked on the hard road. An old bent man felt his way toward the buggy by striking the road with his ironshod staff. "What is it you want?" he asked.

"Who are you?" suspiciously demanded Stella.

"Sostenes Melgosa, at your service," replied Sostenes.

"He has the same name and looks just like the old man you killed back at Cinco Castillos, Cass," said Reata out of the side of his mouth.

"For Christ's sake! Shut up!" snapped Cass. He wiped the cold sweat from his broad face.

166

"We are looking for a man and a small boy," said Stella.

"I heard you ask for them," said Sostenes.

It was very quiet in the sunlit road. The sheep had drifted over a ridge. Now and then a shadow raced along the road when one of the cloud puffs drifted overhead.

"We have seen no such man," said Sostenes.

Basilio Melgosa ran from his great uncle's house and came to stand beside Sostenes. He thrust a small hand into the gnarled hand of the old man.

"By Jesus," murmured Cass. "It's the kid, Stell."

Stella opened her mouth to speak. "Shut up," warned Reata. "Kershaw has been here all right, but for some reason they won't let on he was. For Christ's sake, don't let on you know that."

"Ask him if this road goes through the mountains," said Stella.

"It does," said Reata. "First to Penasco and then to Tres Ritos and Mora."

"What's beyond that?"

"Las Vegas."

"He couldn't have gotten past us on the road

to get back to Santa Fe or to Taos. He's heading for Las Vegas. Drive on, Cass."

Cass picked up the reins. He did not move. The road behind Sostenes had slowly begun to fill with men.

"Is there another way through these mountains to Las Vegas?" asked Stella.

"Back about ten miles," replied Reata.

"We'll lose time going back. Drive on, Cass."

Cass got deliberately out of the buggy. He walked back to his horse. "I'll see you in Las Vegas, Stell," he said. "*If* you make it."

"What the hell is the matter with you two?" she demanded. "Two big men with guns afraid of a handful of greasers standing in the road without so much as a rock in their hands."

"That's what bothers me," said Reata. "The whole damned road is covered with *pedernales*. You ever see a man get hit in the face with one of them?"

"It would be better to go back the way you came!" called out Sostenes.

"That's the warning, Stell," said Reata. "You drive up that road, and maybe you'll never be seen again. They're covering up for Kershaw."

"I'll go where I damn well please!" she snapped. "There are laws in this Territory!"

168

"That is so," agreed Sostenes. He looked toward the angry woman with his milk-white eyes. "But," he quietly added, "we do not see much of the law in this remote area."

How she hated to give in! The thin lines at the side of her lipless mouth drew down, and her curious blue eyes became fixed. "Turn the damnged buggy, Cass!" she cried out through her fury.

Cass walked to the head of the team. He turned them around on the road and the shoulder with the hoofs and wheels grating on the *pedenrales*. Cass got into the buggy and gathered the reins in his big hands. He slapped the reins on the dusty rumps of the team and drove toward the men who filled the road. They parted, making just enough room for the team and buggy, followed by the mounted man, to pass through them. Their brown faces were enigmatic. Reata whistled slightly off key as he passed them. He looked back from a bend in the road. The road was empty. The tightly shuttered houses seemed to look blindly at the road. The *morada* squatted on its knoll. There was no one in sight. It was like an abandoned village. Reata knew better. He did not look back again.

18

THERE was something different and unusual about the windmill in the center of the Las Vegas Plaza. The night wind that swept through the plaza raised the dust and set something in motion alongside the windmill. Lee kneed the tired dun over toward the windmill. The plaza seemed deserted. Only the lights in the windows of the stores and other buildings surrounding the plaza gave any indication that there were people there.

Lee turned his head as he neared the windmill and found himself looking at a pair of booted feet swaying in the night wind. Lee looked up at the body, its neck and head bent at an awkward angle by the noose that had strangled the life out of it. A whitish rectangle showed on the breast. Lee stood up in the stirrups and snapped a match into flame, shielding it in a cupped hand to read the inscription on the card. "Cold-Deck Jim," Lee read aloud. "He was warned to stay out of Las Vegas. He came back. Our loss is Hell's gain. The Vigilantes." The wind blew out the match.

"Who are you?" the hard voice asked from behind Lee.

Lee turned in the saddle. A dozen men stood in the darkness. The lamplight from a nearby building shone dully on the barrels of rifles and shotguns. "Who are *you*?" asked Lee in return.

"Vigilantes," replied the big man closest to Lee.

"I'm passing through," said Lee.

"Maybe you are, and maybe you aren't."

The wind swayed the lynched body so that the boot toes tapped the small of Lee's back.

"Maybe you didn't read the placard we posted here the other day?" suggested the big man.

"Hardly," said Lee drily. "I just now got here."

The man handed Lee a placard. Lee lighted a match. "Notice to thieves, thugs, fakirs, and bunco-steerers among whom are J. J. Harlin, alias Off Wheeler, Saw Dust Charlie, Wm. Hedges, Billy the Kid, Billy Mullin, Little Jack the Cutter, Pock-marked Kid, Cold-Deck Jim Nelson and his partner The Las Vegas Kid, and about twenty others: if found within the limits of this city after ten o'clock P.M. this night, you will be invited to attend a grand necktie party, the expense of which will be borne by one hundred substantial citizens." He blew out the match. "This hardly refers to me," he said.

"We don't know about that. Who are you?"

"The name is Lee Kershaw."

"The manhunter?"

Lee nodded.

"He's lying, Sam," a bearded man said. "I used to know Lee Kershaw. He was killed down in Sonora last year."

The boot toes tapped insistently at Lee's back.

"Get down off that horse," ordered Sam.

Lee dismounted. A match was snapped into light and held close to Lee's face. "You sure, Kelly?" asked Sam.

"Positive! That ain't Kershaw!"

"Who's marshal here now?" asked Lee.

"Tom Bassett," said Sam.

"He knows me," said Lee.

"Come on, then," said Sam.

Lee led the dun after the big man. The Vigilantes walked behind the dun. "I *know* he ain't Kershaw," insisted Kelly.

Lee tethered the dun outside of the marshal's

172

office. Sam opened the door. He looked at Lee as Lee walked past him. "He'd better know you, mister," he warned. He closed the door behind Lee. Lee glanced back over his shoulder through the glass panel of the door. Several of the Vigilantes were lighting up, but their eyes were on the door.

"Marshal!" called out Sam.

Heavy footsteps sounded in the hall that led to the cells. A heavy set man looked at Sam. "What's up, Sam?" he asked.

Sam jerked a head at Lee. "You know this man?"

Bassett looked at Lee. "For the love of God!" he cried out. "Lee! Lee Kershaw! What the hell are you doing in Las Vegas."

Lee felt for the makings. "Passing through, Tom. Just passing through," he said quietly.

Sam grinned. "Sorry, Kershaw," he said.

Lee nodded. "What would have happened to me if Tom here hadn't known me?"

Sam shrugged. "You read the placard," he replied. He closed the outer door behind himself.

Lee sat down. "What's this all about?" he asked.

Tom took a bottle and glasses from a drawer.

"The citizens got tired of the scum that poured in here with the coming of the Santa Fe Railroad. Las Vegas became a catchall for some of the worst rascals and cutthroats in the West. I couldn't keep up with them. The Vigilantes posted a notice; a warning to all that type to steer clear of Las Vegas. It worked."

"I saw some of the result," said Lee drily. "Cold-Deck Jim."

"He was one of the worst. He was here long before the Vigilantes gave him notice, and he figured he'd be big enough to stick it out. He was wrong."

Lee lighted up. "One of the Vigilantes claimed he knew of me. Said I was killed in Sonora last year."

Tom nodded. "The story was passing around. What are you doing up this way? You usually work along the border."

"Looking for a man," said Lee.

"Can I help?"

Lee took out the address book he had taken from the bedroom of Doña Luz. He thumbed across the pages to the only person listed with a Las Vegas address—James H. Nelson, c/o General Delivery, Las Vegas, New Mexico

174

Territory. "James Nelson," said Lee. He looked at Tom. "You know him?"

Tom grinned. "Do I *know* him? You must be joshing!"

"I was never more serious in my life."

Tom shrugged. "You saw the body hanging from the windmill?"

"Cold-Deck Jim?" asked Lee.

"His full name was James Hitchcock Nelson, alias Cold-Deck Jim."

"My luck is running true to form," murmured Lee. "Do you know of a younger man around here whose last name is Diaz?"

"It's not an unusual name around here. What's his first name?"

"Possibly Bart," replied Lee.

"An odd combination of names, Anglo and New Mexican."

Lee nodded. "His father was Anglo. His mother was named Rafaela Diaz. She is a *genizaro* from the Las Trampas area."

Tom shook his head. "It doesn't ring a bell."

Lee emptied his glass. Tom refilled it. "Why is he wanted?" the marshal asked.

"It's not for any crime, Tom. It's a matter of inheritance. His father wants to find him. He hasn't seen his son for eighteen years."

175

"Sounds like a good story."

Lee nodded. "I haven't the time to tell you about it, Tom. This Cold-Deck Jim—what about him?"

"About fifty years of age. Came originally from Missouri. Served in the army here in New Mexico Territory. Got his discharge and drifted into Las Vegas. Never seemed to have to work for a living. He was a gambler, pimp, and general all round bad apple."

"Where'd he get his money?" asked Lee.

"Every month a letter came for him from Santa Fe. That would be the occasion for a three day drunk. He usually ended up here in the *calabozo*. I usually let him go when he was sober—and dead broke."

"This partner of his—the Las Vegas Kid— what about him?"

Tom eyed Lee curiously. "He's about twenty-two or twenty-three years of age. Dark hair and light eyes. Some say he's actually the son of Cold-Deck. Others say the Kid drifted to him from somewhere and Cold-Deck raised him." Tom grinned. "Some upbringing."

Lee twisted another cigarette together. "Where was Nelson stationed in the Army?"

"Fort Marcy at Santa Fe, I think. Yes, that was it."

A little piece of the puzzle slipped into place. "Do you know where the Las Vegas Kid is now?" asked Lee.

Tom stood up. He took a cell key from a rack. "Come on," he offered. "I'll show him to you."

Lee stared at the marshal. "You mean he's here in jail?"

Tom nodded. "I had to lock him up for his own good. The Kid was never anything like his partner Cold-Deck, but he was heading for the same end. He came back into town with Cold-Deck, and Cold-Deck was strung up. I locked the Kid up. I figured I'd slip him out of town when things quietened down a little."

"You say Cold-Deck might have raised the Kid?"

"The Kid had been with Nelson as far back as I can remember."

Lee walked into the cell block after Bassett. All of the cells were empty with the exception of the last one.

Lee looked into the cell. A young man lay full length on a bunk with his interlaced fingers locked at the nape of his neck. His gray eyes flicked at Bassett. "You letting me out of here, Bassett?" he asked.

Bassett shrugged. "It depends on this man here, Kid."

The gray eyes studied Lee. "Who are you?" asked the Kid.

Lee studied the lean and handsome face of the Kid. There was a mingled resemblance there—the dark hair and complexion of the *genizaro* blood and the gray eyes and strong nose of Duke Bowman. "I can get you out of here, Kid," said Lee. "If you want to go."

"Where to?" asked the Kid suspiciously.

Lee looked at Tom. He winked at the marshal with the eye away from the Kid. "He answers to the description, Tom," he said.

"What the hell is this?" demanded the Kid.

"Open the door, Tom," said Lee. He walked into the cell after Tom opened the door. He looked at the marshal. "I'd like to talk with him alone," he suggested. The footfalls of the marshal sounded in the hall. The door closed behind Bassett.

The Kid sat up and rested his lean and graceful hands on each side of himself. Lee handed him the makings. The Kid expertly rolled a cigarette. Lee lit it for him.

178

"*Gracias*," murmured the Kid.

"*Por nada*," countered Lee. He sat in the one rickety chair in the cell.

The Kid blew a smoke ring. "Who are you?" he asked.

"U.S. Marshal," lied Lee. "Looking for a man like you on a federal charge."

"Lets me out," said the Kid. He grinned. "Now, if you had said a county charge, or a city charge, you might have the right man."

"I want to know something of your background," said Lee.

The Kid shrugged. "There isn't much."

"Was Jim Nelson your father?"

The Kid shook his head. "Sort of like a guardian, I'd say."

"Legally?"

"I never saw any papers, if that's what you mean."

"Where were you born?"

"In New Mexico. I don't know the exact place."

"What's your earliest memory?"

The Kid looked curiously at Lee. "You a doctor of some kind?" he asked. "Maybe a fortune teller? You want to read my plam?"

"You didn't answer my question."

179

The Kid looked at the tip of his cigarette. "I was sleeping. There was a lot of shooting. Dead people lying on the ground all bloody. Smoke rising from burning buildings. A lot of yelling. Indians gutting a mule and cooking the meat." His voice died away.

Lee shaped a cigarette. "Go on," he urged.

"The Indians took me up into the mountains. I don't remember much about that except that I liked it there. Then one day an old man came to get me."

"A priest?"

The Kid nodded.

"You remember who he was?"

"No. He took me to Santa Fe. He kept me there for a time and then took me somewhere else. A little village in the mountains. One day a soldier came and got me. He took me here."

"That was Jim Nelson?"

The Kid nodded. "After that I stayed with him. He always had money. We moved around a lot in the early days, but he always came back here."

"For what?"

The Kid shrugged. "Money. Someone was always sending him money. He told me it was his pension from the army."

180

"You have no recollection of your mother?"

The Kid shrugged. "I seem to remember a dark-haired woman. I don't know who she was. She always looked at me in a different way than anyone else."

"When was that?"

"I can't remember."

"Was it before you heard the shooting and saw the Indians?"

"I told you that was my first recollection."

"You saw her after that first recollection?"

"Once when I was with the old priest a young woman came to the chapel to pray. The old priest would not let her in. She cried a lot. I never saw her again."

Lee opened the photograph case. He held it out to the Kid. The Kid stared at the photograph. "By God!" he cried. "I think it is her!"

Lee put a finger on the small boy. "And him?"

The Kid shrugged. "He means nothing to me."

Lee took the photograph. "I'm not so sure about that," he said. He held out the silver button. "What about this?"

The Kid looked at the button and then up at Lee. "Look," he said. He opened his coat. His lowcut velvet vest was fastened with three buttons exactly like the one in Lee's hand.

"Where did you get those?" asked Lee.

The Kid looked down at them. "I've had them all my life," he sid. "Once there were six of them. Jim pawned three of them in Santa Fe one time. We had to eat. I kept the others. I've worn them all my life, one way or another. What do they mean to you?"

Lee stood up. "Just a job," he said, He walked to the door and opened it. He looked back. "Wait for me," he said with a grin as he clicked shut the lock.

Lee walked into the office. "He's my man, Tom," he said.

Tom refilled the glasses. "You can have him," he said. "Just don't let him come back here, Lee, or I won't be responsible for him. When will you leave?"

"Tonight. Now."

Tom looked thoughtfully toward the door. "The boys out there might not take too kindly to that."

"Is the Kid that guilty?"

"Mostly by association. Cold-Deck was a good teacher—of the wrong things. Gambling, a little pimping, and other odds and ends."

"I'll take him off your hands then. He won't be back, at least for a long time."

"Fair enough. How can I help you?"

"My horse is about worn out. I'll need two horses, one for me, one for the Kid, I'll lead the dun."

"Where are you heading?"

"The Broken Bow country."

"On horses? At this time of the year? Why don't you take the Santa Fe?"

Lee shook his head. "Can't risk it."

"Why? There's something queer about all this, Lee."

Lee lit a cigarette. "I'll come back someday and tell you the story. One thing more—there may be some people coming through here looking for me. You don't know anything about me, or the Kid. ¿Comprendes?"

Tom nodded. "That story you're going to tell me some day better be a good one. I'll get your horses for you." He walked to the door and looked back. "One thing you'd better know, Lee. The Kid is one of the best men with a sixgun I've ever seen. Don't trust him too far. I know you can take care of yourself, but the Kid is as slick as a greased pig." He closed the door behind himself.

Lee refilled his glass. He took the cell key and walked to the Kid's cell. He opened the door. The Kid got up and came to the door. "I'm getting out?" he asked.

"With me," said Lee. "Is that your wallet lying there on the bunk?" When the Kid turned his head the Mattatuck irons were neatly snapped about his wrists.

"What the hell is this?" he demanded.

"Just a precaution," replied Lee. "I always promise safe delivery."

"You got a warrant for me?"

Lee opened his coat and touched the butt of his Colt. "Sure, Kid! I've got six of them in here, .44/40 and all fresh." He steered the Kid back into the marshal's office.

Tom Bassett came in the back way. "I got the horses, Lee," he said. "Led them and your dun around to the back. The Vigilantes are over on La Calle de la Amargura checking out the whorehouses on a tip from me. I said I heard that Stuttering Tom and Benny the Poet had been seen over there."

Lee led the Kid to the back door. He looked up and down the alleyway. It was dark and empty.

Lee gave the Kid a hand up into the saddle

of a chunky roan. "Where we heading?" asked the Kid.

"Kansas City," replied Lee. He thrust out his hand to Tom. "I won't forget this, Tom," he said. Tom nodded. He held out a gunbelt heavy with a holstered Colt and full cartridge loops.

"This is the Kid's," he said. "I can't rightfully keep it." Lee hung the belt over his saddlehorn.

Lee mounted the bay and picked up the reins of the roan and the dun. He led them from the alleyway and alongside the plaza. The wind was whipping dust across the plaza. The body of Cold-Deck Jim swayed in the blast. Once, the Kid looked back before Lee led the two horses into a narrow side street that headed south.

19

"ALL I know," said Sam, "is that a man who said he was Kershaw came through here last night. Tom Bassett, the marshal, identified him."

"Tall man with reddish hair and beard? Gray eyes. Big nose. Riding a dun?" asked Reata.

"That was him," agreed Sam.

"Where'd he go?" asked Cass.

"He stayed with Tom after we left the marshal's office. We had some business on Church Street—the one called La Calle de la Amargura, the Road off Suffering and Bitterness. That's because all the whorehouses, saloons, and gambling halls are along there. I . . ."

"Where'd he go after he left the marshal's office?" interrupted Stella.

"Why, I ain't rightly sure. I found out later the marshal bought a couple of extra horses for Kershaw. He left the town about eleven o'clock last night."

"Which way did he go?" asked Reata.

"I don't know."

"Was he alone?" asked Stella.

"All I know is that Kershaw said he was passing through. He's a manhunter. There was only one prisoner in the *juzgado*. When Kershaw left, no one saw him go. But, the prisoner was gone too."

"Who was the prisoner?" asked Stella.

"His last name was Nelson, but everyone called him the Las Vegas Kid. I think Kershaw picked him up."

Reata looked at Stella. "What do you think?"

Stella nodded. "It's him all right. Or someone Kershaw may try to pass off as him."

"What are you talking about?" asked Sam.

Reata shook his head. "An old friend, mister. Thanks for the information."

Sam nodded. "Maybe the marshal can help you out!" he called after the three of them as they walked away.

"He'll be heading south," said Stella. "With about a twelve hour start. How far is it, Reata?"

"More than two hundred miles as the crow flies."

She narrowed her great blue eyes thoughtfully. "He'll have to travel slowly because of the heat. He'll have to go from waterhole to

187

waterhole, and some of them will be dry at this time of the year. I'll get a telegram off to Marsh right away. He can have me met at Alamogordo. The next train is due here in about an hour. I might just make it down there ahead of him."

"What about us?" asked Cass.

She opened her purse. "Buy an extra pair of good horses for each of you. Keep pushing on after him. You might never catch up with him, but you can maybe run him into the net Marsh and I will have ready for him when he gets near the Broken Bow."

Reata shook his head. "We'll never catch up with him," he said.

"Not with Kershaw," said Stella. "But whoever that is with him, Nelson, or the Las Vegas Kid, or whoever the hell he is, might not be able to keep up with Kershaw. Kershaw will be limited to the Kid's endurance, not his own."

Reata nodded. "Yeah," He said slowly.

Cass looked uncertainly to the south. "Jesus, Stell," he said. "That's some ride you got cut out for us."

"You'll make it," she said.

188

"But you ain't never been out there at this time of the year, and in a drought year too!"

She shook her head. "No, and I don't intend to. Now get moving! *Vámonos!* I'll see you at the Broken Bow."

Reata shaped a cigarette as he watched her walking toward the railroad station. "Jesus God," he said quietly. "What a lawman she would have made. She thinks of everything."

Cass spat to one side. "Well, we don't have to do like she says."

Reata looked sideways at Cass as he lit up. "We will if we want to get our hands into a share of the Broken Bow."

Cass nodded. "Let's go get those horses," he said.

As they left the town heading south toward the Pecos, they heard the southbound train whistling for a crossing just outside of Las Vegas.

20

THE key clicked in the lock of the Mattatuck irons. Lee removed them from the Kid's wrists. The Kid rubbed his wrists. "*Gracias*," he murmured, "*mil gracias*."

Lee looked back through the grayness of the dawn light. He fashioned a cigarette and then handed the makings to the Kid. He lit his cigarette. "*Por nada*," he said.

The Kid lit up. "What's your real name, Kershaw?"

Lee looked at him. "Your father wants to see you, Kid."

"I have no father. The only father I ever had is swinging from that windmill back in Las Vegas."

"Your real father is Duke Bowman, of the Running MB in the Broken Bow country. You ever hear of him?"

"Who hasn't?"

"You can have the Broken Bow if you want it, and what is more important—if you can *hold* it."

The Kid studied Lee. "This is loco."

"We'll water the horses two miles from here. That distance should give me just enough time to tell you the whole story," said Lee.

The dawn light came over the open country as they watered the horses. The Kid looked sideways at Lee. "What about my mother?" he asked.

Lee made another cigarette. He lit it.

"You'll have to tell me," the Kid said. "I'll find out anyway when I talk with my father."

"He hasn't seen her for eighteen years," said Lee. "He thinks she's dead."

"But she isn't."

"She is Rafaela Diaz. A *genizaro*. She was supposed to have been killed at Cinco Castillos."

"She came to see me at the chapel in Sante Fe."

Lee nodded. "She's still alive, Kid. I think you know that. I also think you know who she is."

"Cold-Deck got drunk one night after he got my money from her in the mail. He wouldn't give it to me. I took it by force. He tried to cut me down by telling me all about her. He said

191

he'd spread it all over Las Vegas if I took the money."

"But he didn't."

The Kid shook his head. "He would've been dead with a bullet in his rotten guts if he had tried to."

"She was doing it all for you, Kid."

"I would rather have had her dead."

"The damage is done now."

"And the old man? Duke Bowman? The sonofabitch who drove my mother into being a whore? What made him change his mind after all these years."

"Maybe you can guess, Kid."

"He doesn't really give a damn about me personally. All he's really interested in is keeping the Broken Bow away from the Dakins. That's it, isn't it?"

Lee shrugged. "Mine not to reason why. Maybe it's the way he *thinks* he's thinking, Kid. Maybe it's a lot deeper than that. When a man is dying and knows he's dying and still has his reason, a lot of things become clearer. He realizes, perhaps, the importance of other human beings, rather than the possession of material goods."

"You talk like a preacher!" scoffed the Kid.

Lee shook his head. "Read the Bible, Kid. It's all in there."

"And these Dakins? They'll kill to stop us, eh?"

"You've got the idea," admitted Lee.

"Then let me have my gun, Kershaw. I feel naked without it. I've worn it since I was sixteen."

Lee unhooked the belt from his saddlehorn and handed it to the Kid. "You may need it before long," he said.

The Kid settled the belt about his lean hips. "Well, now I feel better. We can take on half a dozen Dakins apiece, eh?"

Lee knelt to fill the canteens. "One apiece is enough," he said quietly.

"You think we're being followed?"

"I know we are."

"Why don't we backtrack and drygulch them?"

"That's not my game, Kid."

"I'll pay you when I take over the Broken Bow."

"Your father is paying me to bring you back there, not to kill your enemies."

"But that used to be your game, didn't it? Bounty hunting?"

Lee capped the first canteen. He would not answer that. The Kid was perceptive enough to know the answer anyway.

"How much do you get for a deal like this?" asked the Kid.

"Usually a thousand for the first week, five hundred a week thereafter. I pay my own expenses. Your father was in a hurry. He doubled the five hundred."

"Maybe you won't make more than a thousand or so."

Lee began to fill the second canteen. "Fill up on water," he suggested. "We've got a long dry ride ahead of us."

"Maybe you have—I haven't," the Kid said quietly.

Lee turned his head slowly and looked up into the handsome face of the Kid.

"I'm not too sure about this deal. It sounds fishy to me. Why are you really doing this?"

"I'm your fairy godfather," drily replied Lee.

"Well, maybe I'll just go down there alone. I don't need you."

Lee shook his head. "No. I'm being paid to deliver you to the old man."

"Maybe it's dead or alive?"

194

Lee stood up and studied the Kid. "You wouldn't do him any good dead, Kid."

"Maybe he just wants me out of the way."

"Then me coming up here after you doesn't make much sense, does it?"

The Kid shook his head. "You're a real pro, Kershaw. You could have killed me up in Las Vegas and maybe have gotten away with it, but you're too smart for that. No, you sprung me out of the *juzgado* and brought me out here where there isn't another soul for miles. Maybe you'll show up at the Broken Bow all alone and collect your blood money, and no one will ever know where I lie buried with a bullet in my back."

"For Christ's sake!" exploded Lee. "I told you to fill up with water! Talking is dry work! Now shut up and drink!"

The Kid slowly shook his head. "You go on alone, Kershaw."

"Drink and get on the roan," ordered Lee.

The Kid smiled, very thinly. "Make me," he suggested.

The sun was shining down on the dry and empty land. Lee looked to the north. There was no sign of dust, which didn't mean anything, for he had swung farther east than the usual waterhole route, which headed south in the straightest line, risking the fact that some of the lesser waterholes would surely be dry.

Lee whirled, drawing his Colt. He found himself looking into the muzzle of the Kid's sixgun. The Kid grinned. "Gotcha!" he crowed.

Lee smiled back. "I hope you don't think I gave you a loaded sixshooter," he suggested. The Kid flicked his eyes uncertainly down at his Colt. A spur jingled. The Colt was slapped hard to one side, spinning out of the Kid's hand, and the muzzle of another Colt was rammed deep into his lean belly just above the belt buckle. The Kid's Colt struck the hard ground and exploded. The soft .44/40 slug struck the roan right between the eyes, and he crashed to the ground.

Lee stepped back. "Get that saddle off the roan, and put it on the bay," he said. "Shift my saddle from the bay to the dun."

The Kid shifted Lee's saddle from the bay to the dun. He unsaddled the fallen roan with Lee's help and then placed the saddle on the bay. He put a foot into the stirrup.

"We walk," said Lee. "It's a long day's trip to the next water."

The sun was already burning up the empty land when the Kid led out the bay. He looked back once at the hard hawk's face behind him and then looked ahead. It was indeed a long day's trip to the next water—if there was any to be had.

21

THE water had a look of stale chocolate about it. Lee raised some of it in his hands and sniffed at it. He dropped the water and wiped his hands on the sides of his trousers. His lips was cracked, and his throat felt like a tube of corroded brass.

"The bay is done," croaked the Kid.

Lee looked at the bay. His legs were spraddled out and gummy yellowish strings hung from his mouth.

"It was your brilliant idea to come this way," accused the Kid. "What now, Kershaw?"

Lee shook the only canteen that had any water in it. He looked across the empty desert country to the southwest. "Cinco Castillos," he said, almost as though to himself.

"How far?" asked the Kid.

"Fifteen miles."

"We'll never make it."

Lee looked at the dying sun, a welter of rose and gold over the distant mountains. "The sun will soon be gone," he said. "That should help a little."

"What about these mysterious people who are supposed to be following us? Maybe they went that way. They could be there now."

"We'll risk it," said Lee. "We have no other choice."

"We should have gone that way in the first place!"

Lee looked sideways at the Kid. "Sometimes," he said quietly, "you run off too much at the mouth."

Lee took off his hat. He poured the last of the water into it and held it out to the dun.

"What the hell are you doing!" exploded the Kid. He rushed at Lee, reaching for the hat. Lee rammed the hat up about the dun's nose, freeing his right hand. He caught the Kid with a backhander that sent him down on one knee. Lee's right heel caught the Kid on the point of the jaw and put him down for the long count.

Lee finished watering the dun. He put the cooled hat on his head and bent down to the place the Mattatucks on the Kid's wrists. He heaved the Kid over the saddle and led the dun toward the southwest and distant Cinco Castillos.

The sun was gone. The darkness was thick. The only sounds on the harsh earth were the scuffling of Lee's moccasins and the thudding of the dun's hoofs, hour after hour, without stop.

The moon came up after a time and touched a curious-looking rock formation placed on the desert like a sand castle built by a child on an empty beach.

"God damn it," husked the Kid. "I'll walk!" Lee gripped the Kid by the belt and pulled him from the tired dun. He yanked the Kid up on his feet and shoved him in the general direction of Cinco Castillos.

Once, the Kid looked back as he stumbled along, into the hawk's face beneath the low pulled hat brim. There was no expression on Lee Kershaw's face.

A mile from Cinco Castillos Lee stumbled and fell. As he tried to get up, the Kid's bootheel caught him on the jaw and he fell back half-stunned. The Kid ripped Lee's Colt from its holster and held it on Lee. "Where's the key?" he demanded. Lee held out the key to him. "Unlock these cuffs," the Kid croaked.

Lee sat up, feeling his bruised jaw. "Try it yourself," said Lee. The Kid took the key and tried to fit it into the keyhole. "I'll hold the Colt for you," suggested Lee.

The moon was bright on the desert. The Kid looked toward Cinco Castillos. He looked down at Lee. "Unlock the cuffs, Kershaw," he said. "Or you don't get any water."

Lee stood up and looked toward the pinnacles. He shook his head.

"What's the matter?" demanded the Kid.

Lee looked at him. "I'm not sure," he said.

"Is there someone there?"

"*¿Quien sabe?*"

"You're bluffing, Kershaw!"

Lee shrugged.

"We can't bypass that water."

"No," admitted Lee. he reached over and unlocked the cuffs. "You'd better wait awhile, Kid," he advised.

"What's the sense of waiting?"

"There may be a reception committee there you won't like."

The Kid waved the Colt. "Lead the dun," he ordered.

Lee picked up the reins. He rubbed his bruised jaw. "You learn fast in some ways, Kid," he said.

Lee led on the tired dun. There could be no

going back. They would never be able to reach the waterhole back north, beyond the one with the poisoned water. They could not bypass Cinco Castillos to try for Ribbon Creek. They were damned if they went to Cinco Castillos and damned if they didn't.

The Kid saw the ruins. He saw the mounded graves, lit by the moon. He saw the passageway that led in to the water. "Get moving!" he snapped. "*Vámonos!*"

Lee dropped the reins. He felt in his shirt pocket for the makings. "I don't like it," he said quietly.

The Kid snatched up the reins. He began to run awkwardly. "Stay there then and die of thirst!" he yelled. The echo flatted off from the pinnacles.

Lee lit the cigarette. The Kid vanished in through the passage. Lee stood there with the smoke doing his thirst no good. He threw the cigarette aside and walked toward the pinnacles. His footfalls sounded in the shadowed passageway. He stopped at the inner opening. A man squatted in the shadows beside the *tinaja* with a cigarette held cupped in his hand. The dun whinnied from the shadows beyond the *tinaja*.

"Maybe you were right after all, Kid," admitted Lee.

The shadowed figure nodded. Lee walked toward the water. The man stood up, drawing in on his cigarette. The flaring tip revealed the broad face and hard green eyes of Cass Dakin. A gun hammer clicked back to full cock. "Kershaw, you sonofabitch," said Cass. "What kept you so long?"

Lee whirled and dived back into the tunnel as Cass fired. The bullet slapped into the tunnel wall and ricocheted back and forth over Lee's head. He rolled over and over and jumped to his feet. He plunged out of the tunnel and hurdled the graves, heading for the ruins.

Hoofs thudded on the hard ground. Lee threw a glance back over his shoulder. A horseman was rounding the pinnacles and whirling a reata over his head. The loop settled neatly about Lee's chest, pinning his arms to his body. The horseman reined back his horse, and the reata tightened, snapping Lee back onto his lean butt; the shock traveled all the way up his back into his brain.

The horse was spurred forward and past Lee. Lee looked up into the grinning face of the rider and managed to get up onto his feet as the reata took up. He ran awkwardly after the horse with the grit and pebbles flung up from the rear hoofs stinging his face.

"Have a nice trip, Kershaw!" roared Cass from the rim between the bases of the pinnacles. "Go to it, Reata!"

Reata turned grinning. "Stay on your feet or die, Kershaw!" he yelled back. "How long do you think you'll last?"

They rounded the pinnacles out of sight of the howling Cass. Reata turned his horse toward the thick masses of thorned brush on the lower ground.

Lee drew his knife and sliced through the loop, but caught and twisted the reata in his left hand keeping up the drag on it. Lee timed his stride. He drew back the knife in his right hand and made a hard cast to save his life. The blade centered itself between Reata's shoulder blades. Lee let go of the reata. The horse took off through the thorned brush with Reata still bolt upright in the saddle. The moonlight glinted on the polished hilt of the knife.

Lee passed a hand across his burning eyes. He looked back at the pinnacles. Cass was not in sight. Lee slogged back toward the pinnacles. He found a place where he could use hand- and footholds to work his way up between two of the pinnacles. He rolled over the rim and lay flat looking down into the *tinaja* area.

"Your friend Kershaw won't be back," said Cass to the Kid.

"He's no friend of mine," said the Kid. "How about untying me?"

"Why?" asked Cass.

"I need a drink."

Cass shaped a cigarette. "You won't be needing it," he said.

Lee picked up a melon-sized rock.

"Kill him now," the mind voice said.

Cass lit his cigarette. "How do you want it? Back, belly, or head?" he asked the Kid.

"Why kill me?" asked the Kid.

"You're old Bowman's bastard, ain't you?"

The Kid shook his head.

"The hell you ain't!"

"What makes you think so?" asked the Kid.

"Because Kershaw wouldn't have brought you this far if he didn't know it, that's why!"

"He's wrong, mister. Bowman's kid was killed right here at Cinco Castillos by the Mescaleros."

"How do you know that?" asked Cass.

"It's common knowledge," replied the Kid.

"No, it ain't. Who the hell would care if the kid *was* killed here? That was eighteen years ago."

"How much do you want to let me go?"

"Make me an offer," suggested Cass.

"A thousand bucks?"

"Have you got it?"

"Not with me."

"Where is it?"

"In Las Vegas."

Cass blew a smoke ring. "Damn," he said. "You know how much the Broken Bow is worth?"

"I haven't any idea."

"Maybe a quarter of a million dollars," said Cass.

"How much of it do you think you'll get?" asked the Kid.

Cass thrust forward his head. "What the hell do you mean?"

"By the time your brother Marsh and your sister Stella get their hands into that property you won't get nothing, mister!"

Cass yawned. "I asked you before—how do you want it? Back, belly, or head?" He drew his Colt.

A strong arm encircled Cass's thick neck, and

the rock came down with savage force against the side of his thick head. The big man clamped his chin down on Lee's arm and swung sideways. The Colt clattered on the hard ground. Lee's feet came up off the ground, and he was swung around. Cass raised his head and Lee fell heavily, knocking the Colt into the *tinaja*.

Cass rubbed the side of his head as he looked down at Lee. "Well, well," he said conversationally. "Where's my cousin Reata?"

"He took a long ride out into the desert," replied Lee. "He won't be back."

"And you come here for a drinka water, eh?"

"You've got the idea," said Lee. He stood up with his back to the pool. There were three horses in the shadows, two of them with sheathed Winchesters on the saddles.

"Looks like it's finally between me and you now, Kershaw," said Cass. "You killed Reata, eh?"

Lee nodded.

"You haven't got a gun, or you would have shot me with it. You haven't got a knife, or it would have been between my shoulder blades. You killed Chisos and Reata by trickery. How are you in a fair fight?"

"Is there such a thing in this business?" asked Lee.

Cass looked down at his huge fists. "Well," he said slowly, "I am a sporting man, Kershaw. You lick me in a fistfight, and I'll let you pass."

"That's fair?" asked Lee.

"Man to man. Ain't *that* fair?"

"He'll kill you, Kershaw," said the Kid.

Lee glanced at him. "If he kills me, Kid, you're next." Lee bent down and scooped up a little water, keeping his eyes on Cass. "By the way, Cass?" he asked. "How did the old man Candelario Melgosa die?"

"I only hit him once," blurted Cass.

Lee stood up straight and tall. He unbuckled his gunbelt with its empty holster. He peeled off his sweat-damp shirt and undershirt to reveal his lean gut and long flat muscles.

Cass stripped to the waist. His muscles bulged, and his chest seemed hewed from solid oak. "Texas rules?" he asked casually.

Lee bowed his head. "Your choice," he said. "He'll kill you, Kershaw," warned the Kid again.

Cass spat to one side. He closed his huge hands and thrust them out, turning the wrists outward so that his fists were presented one behind the other, in front of his block of a chin. He thrust forward a heavy left leg and placed his right foot in line behind it. "Time," he said seriously.

"I don't believe it," murmured the Kid.

"He means it," said Lee.

Lee began to move about just out of range of those dangerous blocks of fists. He threw a probing left and it met a hard forearm. He tried a right cross and hit another forearm. He circled about. "Stand still, you damned jumping jack," muttered Cass.

The right came in a straight jab that knocked Lee's blocking left out of the way and connected solidly with his jaw. He hit the ground and rolled out of the way of the descending boot. He came up on his feet. Cass hit him with a left and then a right, and he went down again. Blood leaked from his mouth. This time the boot caught him in the ribs with a jolt that knocked the wind out of him. He rolled over and Cass jumped, trying to land on his back with both huge feet.

Lee moved back, shaking his head. Cass threw a right. As he did so, he lowered his left. The fist fanned past Lee's jaw. Lee knew that if he went down again, he might not be able to get out of the way of those murderous feet. "Texas rules," Cass had said, and he had meant it.

Cass threw a right. It missed. Again he had lowered his left. He feinted with his left and rammed his right against Lee's belly. Lee's back slammed against the rock wall behind him. He drifted sideways and circled to get out into the open.

Cass shuffled forward throwing rights and lefts, but he didn't seem to be trying very hard to hit Lee, as though playing with him. He lowered his left as he threw a right, and at the same time, he looked toward the Kid. "Any minute now," he said. The hard left speared against his broad nose, and the vicious right came over the top of his lowered left arm and hit him square in the left eye. He grunted and bent forward. A left caught him in his meaty belly, and as he raised his head, the right smashed against his left eye again.

Lee backed away, breathing hard. His throat was dry and his tongue was swollen with thirst. Blood dripped from his abraded knuckles.

Cass pawed at his left eye with his right fist. He shuffled forward. He threw a right which fanned past Lee's jaw. Lee rammed out his left foot and caught the big man hard in the privates. As Cass bent forward in agony, a left smashed against his right eye, and a right almost completely closed his left eye for the evening.

"Time," said Cass.

Lee spat bloodily to one side. "Time, hell," he said. He moved in and hit Cass on his nose and slammed a left into the right eye.

"Goddamn you!" roared Cass. "Fight fair!"

The left just about closed Cass's right eye. A right caught him in the groin. He staggered back. A vicious one-two caught the left eye and then the right eye in turn.

Cass stood still, with his head held tilted back peering through his swollen eyes. Lee was just a lean shadowy figure moving about like a prowling cat, just out of fist range.

Cass lowered his head and thrust out his arms to charge against Lee, driving his hard skull into Lee's belly and throwing his arms about Lee's waist. They went down with Lee under the big man and the breath driven out of his body. He brought up a knee into Cass's groin, and as he felt the relaxation of the big man's grip, he broke free and staggered to his feet.

He got in two good boots to the back of the head before Cass made it to his feet.

They circled each other—the tall, lean man with his fists out, weaving back and forth, and the huge-bodied Cass with his thick arms outspread, trying to see through the hairline slits between his swollen eyelids. Once again he charged. This time the cruel fists slammed into both eyes, and Lee was gone, backing toward the rock wall beside the *tinaja*. "You stink!" jeered Lee. "All you can hit are helpless old men!"

Cass charged, roaring like a mad bull, arms outspread and bull head lowered. Lee side-stepped at the last possible second. Cass rammed his bullet head full force against the rock wall and fell like a chopped tree.

Lee wiped the sweat and blood from his face. He knelt beside the water and scooped it up to his dry mouth. The drippings were like mercury in the bright moonlight.

"Is he still alive?" asked the Kid.

Lee sat down and thrust out his arms on each side of himself. He looked at the swollen face of the big man. The thick chest did not move. "Texas rules," he said quietly. "That was what he wanted."

212

"I'd like a drink," the Kid said.

Lee got to his feet. He untied the Kid and pulled him to his feet. "Help yourself," he said.

They sat there in the moonlight looking at each other.

"The next water south is Ribbon Creek," said Lee.

"How soon will you be able to leave?" asked the Kid.

Lee felt for the makings. "After we have a smoke," he replied.

22

THE KID stumbled and fell flat on his face. He did not try to get up; he did not even move.

"Keep moving," came the inexorable command.

The Kid got to his feet by a supreme effort of will. He thrust out a hand as though to balance himself, but he could not take another step.

"Stop posing," came the suggestion from behind the Kid. "Keep moving!"

The Kid turned and looked through the predawn darkness at the inhuman creature behind him.

"Keep moving, or you'll die here," said Lee.

"What keeps *you* moving?" he asked.

"Meanness," replied Lee. "Some people have determination; others have faith; me—Kershaw —I'm just *mean*. Keep moving!"

The Kid *moved*.

A faint grayish tint showed in the eastern sky.

"How much farther?" asked the Kid.

The dun whinnied sharply.

Lee gripped the Kid by a shoulder and dragged him backward.

They stood there in the darkness. Lee raised his head.

"What's the matter?" asked the Kid. A big dirty hand was clamped over his mouth.

The dawn light grew. The canyon wrens twittered sleepily, and then they stopped. There was no wind.

Lee looked up the slopes toward the great ridge that trended north, sawtoothed against the dark gray sky.

"Where's the water?" husked the Kid when Lee took his hand away.

The hand came right back again. Lee pulled his Winchester from its scabbard. He leaned close to the Kid. "Unsaddle the dun," he said. He vanished into the woods.

The Kid unsaddled the dun and drew his Colt.

A rifle exploded in the darkness. The echo was immediately chased by the echoes of half a dozen shots sounding like the sporadic ripping of heavy canvas. Smoke drifted through the graying darkness.

Lee came loping through the woods. He handed the smoking Winchester to the Kid.

215

"Shoot that way!" he snapped, jerking his head. He ripped open a saddle bag and stuffed something inside his shirt. The Kid opened fire and ran the Winchester dry.

"Now!" said Lee. He dumped the saddle between some rocks and kicked brush over it. He ran lightly up the slope—not as though he had just walked for twelve hours straight across the dry country north of Ribbon Creek.

"Kershaw!" yelled a man. He stood up in the dimness and raised his rifle. Lee turned sideways, drawing as he did so, and fired from hip level. The man went down and rolled into cover, still firing. The slugs slapped through the woods cutting down twigs and striking into trunks.

Men yelled back and forth. Boots splashed in water. A horse whinnied in sudden panic.

The Kid slogged up the slope after Lee. His breathing was like that from the bellows of a forge. His legs quivered with the strain of working up the rugged slope. He fell over a log. He cracked a shin against a rock.

"Keep moving!" yelled Lee. He turned once and emptied his Colt right over the top of the Kid's head. He reached down and gripped the

216

Kid by the gunbelt and half carried and half dragged him higher and higher.

Lee rolled over a slantways dike of rock and fell flat on his face with the Kid atop him. The fresh sweat broke out and brought alive the stale odor of the past several days' perspiration. Their lungs seemed to be on fire.

"Load the Winchester," ordered Lee. He shoved his hat back to let it hang from its strap and raised his head a little. He went down at once. A slug slapped the place where his head had showed.

Lee placed his back against a rock and felt for the makings. He grinned at the Kid. "Close, that," he observed.

"Broken Bow men?"

Lee nodded. He placed the cigarette between the Kid's lips and swiftly rolled another quirly for himself. He lit both cigarettes.

The faint sounds of shouting men came from the slopes below. They lay there resting and smoking. Minutes ticked past.

The sun shoved up its fat round face over the mountains far to the east. The heat seemed to come at once.

"Maybe they were just out hunting strays?" the Kid suggested.

Lee nodded. "Sure are—*us*." Lee pointed to a V between the rock dike and a huge boulder. "Take a look down that way, Kid," he said. "That might all be yours some day. Keep your head low."

The Kid bellied to the V and looked down the long tumbled slopes of barren rock to the lower timber-covered slopes. The sun glinted from the ripples of Ribbon Creek. To the right, southeasterly, he saw a great, dark curving line —the Broken Bow.

"The *estancia* is up the valley," explained Lee. "We can't see it from here."

"What happens now?"

"We go to see your father."

"From up here? There ain't no water above us. We can't get over that damned mountain there to the valley. We can't go down and get water. You let the dun go."

Lee scratched inside his shirt. "Have faith," he said drily. "We can climb better and faster than the horse. Besides, I didn't want to risk having the dun break a leg. By God! You ever see a horse like that dun? He outlasted them all!"

The Kid crawled back under the cover of the

dike. "Helluva lot of good that'll do! They've got him now."

"They'll never keep him. I'll find him around Ribbon Creek on my way out of the Broken Bow."

The Kid rested his sweating back against the dike. He looked at the hawk's face across from him, with its hard gray eyes, big nose, mahogany-hued skin, and reddish beard. He saw the bruises from Lee's fight with Cass Dakin—Texas rules. He saw the mark where he had kicked Lee. He watched the lean hands molding a cigarette with swift and skillful precision. He heard the sounds of hunting men coming closer up the slopes below them. "Don't you ever give up?" he asked.

Lee shook his head as he placed the cigarette between the Kid's cracked lips. He lit it. "Nope," he said. "They'll have to kill me first." It was not bravado with Lee Kershaw; just a simple statement of fact.

Lee lit his own cigarette. He leaned back against the rock and closed his eyes.

"You think of everything," observed the Kid.

Lee shook his head. "Not everything," he corrected.

"Such as?"

"I have no way of foreseeing what will happen when I get you to the *estancia* to see your daddy."

"But we *will* see him?"

Lee opened his eyes. "Why of course! What makes you doubt it?"

The Kid had no comment on that question.

Lee snubbed out his cigarette. "Give me a hand," he said.

Together they worked a boulder over just to the end of the rock dike. Lee braced his back against another boulder and his feet against the one they had moved. "You want to sight it?" he asked. The Kid stared at him. Lee shoved with all his force. The boulder rolled downward, and as it gained speed, it struck a downslanted sheet of rock and took off like a giant billiard ball into the bright morning sunlight.

Lee jumped to his feet. "Look out below!" he yelled through cupped hands.

They could hear yelling, cursing men below them on the slopes. "Goddamn you, Kershaw!" yelled Sid Dakin.

Lee grinned like a hunting lobo on a moonlit night when he sees his prey. "Lookit them run!

Hey, Marsh! Raise your ass a little higher when you hurdle and put out your arms so!" Here Lee made an exaggerated pose with left arm outflung and right arm and leg straight behind him. A bullet slapped viciously into the rock dike.

Lee stepped behind the dike. "Time to move, Kid. It'll take them a while to catch their breaths. Their shooting will be wild and uphill. Now, you might not know, but when a man shoots uphills, he has a tendency to shoot too low, and when he shoots downhill, he has a tendency to overshoot." Lee kept on his impromptu lecture as he worked his way up a transverse cleft in the rock. The sound of the rolling, bounding boulder, accompanied by the clattering, rushing sound of loose rock and soil, died away. Dust wreathed up from far below, accompanied by the verbal smoke of the cursing Broken Bow men.

The sun beat on the eastward side of the huge ridge. The heat veils shimmered upward from the baking rock. There was no wind to move the heavy masses of inert air.

The Kid looked far down the shimmering slope and saw the glinting of the sun on the narrow ribbon of the creek. He looked toward the looping Broken Bow, flowing steadily down to meet the Pecos in the heat-hazed distance. He looked back over his shoulder at Lee taking a break in the hot shadow of a huge boulder. "We can't outlast them, Kershaw," he said.

Lee opened his eyes. "So, what solution do you have?"

"Go on down there and give ourselves up."

Lee took a shapeless mass of soft candle wax out of his shirt front and rolled it in his hands to reshape it into a candle. "Evidently you haven't got the idea," he suggested. "That's Sid Dakin down there, *segundo* to his brother Marsh, who ramrods the Broken Bow. Now, Sid never got to be *segundo* just because he hapened to be Marsh's half brother, Kid. Sid is lazy as hell, except when it comes to a gunfight or a shooting scrape—then he's all horns and rattles. Sid has his orders from Marsh and his sister Stella—the Black Widow. His orders are to kill the both of us. You, because you're the heir to the Broken Bow. Me, because I *know* you're the heir to the Broken Bow. Sonny, they don't ever intend for us to leave this mountain alive."

The Colt hammered clicked back. Lee looked up into the muzzle of the sixgun and stopped shaping the second candle. "Jesus," he said. "Are we back in that act again?"

The Kid looked down at Lee over the Colt. "I'm going down. I can reason with them. We can't live up here in this heat without any water. The farther we get away from Ribbon Creek, the quicker we die."

Lee placed the candles in the shade and felt for the makings. "I really ought to stop you now," he said.

"You think you can?"

The gray eyes looked steadily over the Colt. "Don't doubt it," replied Lee drily. "However, I'm tired of saving your ass from those buzzards down there. You go right ahead, sonny. You *reason* with them. Two things—leave the Winchester, please, and don't bother to let me know how you make out. I'll hear the shooting."

The Kid let down the hammer of the Colt. "What are you going to do with those candles?" he asked.

Lee shrugged. "I'll place one at your head and the other at your feet when they get through with you down there."

"That's not funny," said the Kid.

"It's not intended to be funny."

Lee lit his cigarette. He reached for the Winchester and levered a round into the chamber. He let the hammer down to half cock and looked slantways up at the Kid. "I'm ready when you are," he said.

The Kid let down the hammer of his Colt and sheathed it. He turned on a heel and threw a leg over a rock ledge. He stepped over it into the full sunlight and began to walk stiff-legged down the slope, braking himself on the loose soil and rock.

It was very quiet on the mountainside. Lee slowly slid the Winchester barrel between two rocks, making sure the sun did not reflect from the metal. He eased back on the spur hammer, full cocking the rifle.

"Hey, Dakin!" yelled the Kid. "I'm coming down!"

There was no answer.

The Kid looked back up the slope. He saw nothing. The heat shimmered up sinuously, almost as though in an obscene dance from some Oriental bagnio.

"Hey, you!" Sid Dakin yelled. The echo fled down the mountainside and died away.

The Kid looked toward a huge tip-tilted slab of rock half buried in the talus slope just below him. A man stood there, out of sight of Lee Kershaw. He held a Winchester in his hands. The muzzle was pointed toward the Kid.

The Kid stopped walking. He turned slowly to face Dakin. There were other men hidden here and there on the slope, but they were not watching the Kid. Their half-slit eyes were looking over their gun barrels, through the buckhorn sights and over the knifeblade front sights, waiting for a clear shot at the wolf-man who was hidden high above them.

"Are you really Bowman's bastard?" asked Sid.

"He's not my father," said the Kid.

"Then why did Kershaw bring you back here?"

The Kid smiled a little. "You know Kershaw," he said.

Sid nodded. "I know Kershaw. That's why I think you must be Bowman's bastard."

Hot sweat worked down the Kid's sides. The rock burned up through his worn bootsoles as though he was standing on a griddle. The heat waves shimmered and swayed, and the hard face of Sid Dakin seemed to go into focus and out of it again. "Look, Dakin," said the Kid. "Let me pass. I'll get a drink down at the creek and keep on going. That's what it is all about, isn't it? I won't come back."

Dakin looked sideways at a man standing behind a boulder watching upslope toward Kershaw. "You hear that, Cousin Ben?" he asked. "He won't come back . . . ."

"He's got that right, anyway," said Cousin Ben.

Dakin raised his rifle. "Get rid of that Colt," he ordered.

The Kid dropped his hand to his Colt. He jumped sideways and dropped. "Shoot, Kershaw!" he yelled.

Dakin jumped out into clear to get a shot at the Kid. The Winchester high on the slope cracked flatly. Dakin spun about, dropped the Winchester, and staggered back behind the slab of rock. The second shot's echo chased the first. Cousin Ben went down with a bullet in his left shoulder. Dakin gripped his right shoulder with a dirty left hand. Blood leaked between his fingers. "Get the bastard!" he yelled. "Get the bastard! Get the bastard!" echoed and re-echoed the mountain.

A faint wraith of gunsmoke drifted high on the slope. There was no one in sight. Nothing moved except the shimmering heat veils.

The Kid lay belly-flat on the burning ground with a bout six inches of rock higher than his shoulders and butt and with his face pressed against the ground. He slanted his eyes sideways and looked up the slope. The place seemed as barren and deserted as a lunar landscape.

"Go get him!" yelled Sid crazily at his *vaqueros*.

No one went to get *him*; no one moved.

When darkness came over the burning land, Lee heard a faint scraping, rustling noise. He sat up and reached for the Winchester.

"It's me," croaked the Kid.

Lee dragged him over the rock dike. "Get on your feet," he ordered.

"I'm burned to a crisp," groaned the Kid.

Lee hooked a hand under the Kid's collar. He dragged him to his feet. "When the moon comes up, it'll be like daylight on these slopes. We've got tracks to make before then."

The Kid thrust his burned face close to the hawk's face, dim under the hat brim. "To where, Goddamn you! There ain't no water up there! There ain't nothing up there but death, you ornery bastard!"

227

"You want to go back down there again?" asked Lee.

The Kid turned and began to climb up through the darkness.

The moon tinted the eastern sky. The moonlight grew across the country east of the Pecos.

"Listen," hissed Lee.

The Kid stopped and looked down the slope. A rock was clattering somewhere in the dimness below them.

When the moonlight bathed the great barren slopes, there was no sign of Kershaw and the Kid.

A man gingerly peered over the sheer edge of the escarpment. "Jesus, Al," he said over his shoulder. "That's at least a two thousand foot drop down to the slopes."

Al grounded his Winchester and wiped the sweat from his burning face. "They ain't up here, Carl. That's all there is to it."

Carl looked back down the great eastern slopes, now bright in the moonlight. "We're the only ones got up to the top," he said. He looked sideways at Al. "What the hell we goin' to tell Sid when we get back down there?"

"Not a Goddamned thing," said Al. "Because, brother, I ain't going back down there. In fact, I ain't ever going back to the Broken Bow, and if you've got any Goddamned sense at all, you won't either. Not while Kershaw is still around. I want no part of that devil."

They walked together back down the slope. In a little while, the sound of their voices and that of the clattering rock was faint in the distance.

Lee stepped out from behind a rock. "Come on, Kid," he said.

The Kid walked like an automaton behind the lean shape of Lee Kershaw.

"Here," said Lee. He pointed to a dark opening in the rock wall. He waved a dirty hand. "Open, Sesame!" he cried. He led the Kid by an arm into the cave. He lit one of his reshaped candles and held it up. "Aladdin's cave, Kid. Beyond it are the riches of the universe for you." He led the way into the winding passage with the cool draft playing about their burning faces.

Lee stopped in the great, domed room and lit the second candle. He stuck each of them on a separate stalagmite and gestured toward the emerald pool. "The Waters of Nepenthe," he said.

The Kid fell flat on his belly, and his face went under the clear cold water. He raised his head when he had drunk. "There is a madness in you, Kershaw," he said.

Lee rolled the last of the tobacco into two cigarettes. He placed one in the mouth of the Kid and one in his own. He lit them with one of the candles. "We've got a few hours until the moon passes over the mountains to the west," he said, "Then I'll take you home, Kid."

23

DUKE BOWMAN sat in his heavy rawhide-covered chair and stared into the flickering, shifting kaleidoscope of color hovering over the thick bed of embers in the beehive fireplace. His big liver-spotted hands rested almost lifelessly on the hardwood arms of the chair. Slowly he raised his head. He turned to face the slight draft that suddenly blew into the room from an opened window.

The shadowy figure in the corner spoke softly: "What do you see in the color painting of the embers, Duke?"

"Kershaw?" asked Duke.

"I've brought someone home, Duke," said Lee.

The Kid walked toward his father. The dull eyes of the old man looked up into the firelit face of the son he had never really known.

Lee dropped into a chair close to the draped front window and handy to the liquor cabinet and Duke Bowman's fine clear Havanas. He finger-parted the drapes so that he could see down toward the shadow-darkened river and the pale ribbon of graveled road that came up the valley from the east. He poured a drink of brandy and lit a cigar. He could hear the murmuring voices of the two men, father and son, but he wasn't interested in what they were saying.

"Kershaw," said the old man.

Lee looked up.

"Bart will need your help to take over the Broken Bow," said the old man.

Lee shook his head. "My job is done, Bowman. I'm a manhunter, not a paid gun."

"I didn't know you had any principles in that respect," sneered Bowman.

Lee blew out a smoke ring and watched it lift and waver in the draft. "The Kid can take care of himself," he said.

"Against those killers! He wouldn't have a chance!"

Lee looked between the drapes. "What killers?" he asked over his shoulder.

"Why, Marsh, Sid, Cass, Chisos, Reata, and some of the others, like Nuno Mercado!"

Lee turned. "Chisos is dead with a bullet in his heart. Nuno Mercado is buried in an unmarked grave near Santa Fe. Reata died with a knife between his shoulder blades. Cass butted out what little brains he had. Sid is up near Ribbon Creek with a bullet in his right shoulder. Cousin Ben has one in the left shoulder."

The old man blinked his eyes. "Who killed them?" he asked.

Lee refilled his glass. "It wasn't your son," he replied.

Bowman looked at the Kid. "It still leaves Marsh and some of his boys."

The Kid looked at Lee. "What about him?" he asked.

"I'm willing to bet his boys have left him. You'll have to face him down, Kid."

Bowman stared at Lee. "Are you loco? Marsh will kill him!"

Lee looked at the Kid. "He can take care of himself, Duke."

"I'll go instead!"

Lee shook his head. "No, Duke. He has to do it himself."

The Kid drew his Colt and checked the loads. He snapped shut the loading gate.

Hoofs sounded on the graveled road. Lee peered through the parting of the drapes. A lone horseman was riding toward the great limestone *casa*. He looked up at the tower.

Lee let the drapes fall together. "He's down there now, Kid," he said over his shoulder. He stood up and refilled his glass. He downed the good brandy and wiped his mouth. Putting some cigars into a shirt pocket, he walked toward the rear window.

"Where the hell are you going?" asked Duke.

Lee turned when he reached the window. "My job is done," he said. "It's up to the Kid now, Duke."

The old man opened and then closed his mouth. He looked quickly at the Kid. When he looked back toward the window, Lee had vanished.

"Let him go," said the Kid.

"Marsh and his boys will cut you down," warned Duke.

The Kid shook his head. "Marsh will be alone, Duke."

"What makes you think so?"

The Kid lit a cigarette. "Marsh is probably the only one of them who's not afraid of Kershaw."

Duke gripped the arms of his chair. "Good luck, son," he said. He did not look around as

234

the door closed behind the Kid. He heard the soft husking of the bootsoles on the stone steps and then the quiet closing of the lower tower door.

24

MARSH DAKIN turned suddenly in his stride as he walked toward the lamplit log *casa*. "Who're you?" he demanded.

The Kid walked forward into the rectangle of light from one of the windows. "The name is Bowman," he replied. "Bart Bowman."

Marsh stared at him. "The bastard?"

The Kid nodded.

"How'd you get in here?"

"Kershaw," replied the Kid.

Marsh nodded. "I can't believe it."

"I'm here," said the Kid simply.

Marsh glanced up toward the tower. "You talked with the old man?"

The Kid nodded.

Marsh smiled thinly. "And he sent you down here to take over?"

"You're getting the idea," agreed the Kid.

Marsh slowly rubbed his jaw. "I've got half a dozen *vaqueros* within shouting distance," he said.

The Kid shook his head. "You're all alone, mister."

"So, then it's finally between me and you?"

"There's no one else here," replied the Kid.

"Where's Kershaw?"

"Gone like he came—unseen by anyone."

"And yellow as a canary!"

The Kid shook his head. "He did his job."

"Maybe you should have sent him to face me down."

The Kid smiled. "That wasn't necessary."

Marsh telegraphed his intent by moving his head a little. The Kid gripped the rim of his hat and sailed it towards Marsh's face. Marsh averted his face but drew and fired where the Kid had been standing. The Kid had jumped sideways and turned halfway in a crouch to fire from waist level. Marsh dropped his smoking Colt to grip his right forearm with his left hand. Shock was on his face. Blood dripped between his left fingers. The double echo of the shooting died away up the dark canyon of the Broken Bow.

The Kid picked up his hat. He picked up Marsh's Colt and thrust it under his gun belt. "Let me take a look at that arm," he suggested.

Marsh shook his head. "The bullet went

clean through," he said. He took out his bandanna and tied it about the forearm, drawing the knot tight with his teeth. "You could have killed me," he said. "Why didn't you?"

"I've never killed a man," the Kid said simply, "and I didn't want to start now."

Marsh nodded. "Fair enough," he said. "I'll take my horse. He's my own, Bowman."

Marsh walked toward the log *casa*. He opened the door. The Kid followed him into the large living room. Stella Dakin sat in a chair beside the table. She wore her basque traveling coat and her ridiculous hat with the dusty bird atop it staring at the world with its glassy eyes.

"She's all ready to travel, Marsh," said Lee easily. He sat in a chair tilted back against the wall. A cigar was stuck in the side of his mouth, and his lean face was wreathed in thin smoke. He never took his eyes away from Stella.

Marsh looked at his sister. "It's all over, Stell," he said.

"You botched the deal," she said thinly.

The Kid studied her. He looked at Lee. Lee nodded. "She's the real enemy, Kid," he said.

"I've got something coming to me!" she shrilled.

"You sure have," said Lee drily. He relit his cigar. "The old man is slowly dying, Marsh," he said. He looked up at the foreman. "You know why?"

"I haven't any idea," said Marsh.

Lee let the chair tilt forward. He stood up. "Ask her," he suggested. He looked at the Kid. "Come on, Kid."

Marsh held up his left hand. "Wait," he siad. "You've started something here, Kershaw. You'd better finish it."

"Did you know how her first husband died?" asked Lee.

Her eyes were fixed and set. The thin wire-like lines at the corners of her mouth drew down hard. "He's lying, Marsh," she said.

Marsh looked at her. "I wonder," he said.

"Duke Bowman has only a few months to live," put in Lee. "Remember how he used to be, Marsh? Up until five years ago, he could take on any man of his *corrida* with fist and boot. Now, look at him."

Marsh looked at his sister with horror. "I never believed that story about your first husband," he said slowly.

"He's lying!" she repeated.

Lee jerked his head at the Kid. They walked

239

outside. They could hear the rising voices from within the log *casa*.

"What is it, Lee?" asked the Kid.

Lee looked up at the tower where Duke Bowman waited for slow death. "They called her the Black Widow once," he said. He looked at the Kid. "They breed with the male and then poison him so the young can live off his body." He looked toward the house. He shook his head. "I'll need a horse," he said.

"Take your pick," said the Kid.

"I'll go look for my dun."

"How much does the old man owe you?"

"About a thousand," replied Lee.

"I'll go get it."

Lee shook his head. He walked toward the corral. "You can mail it to me, Kid, when you get around to it."

Marsh banged open the door of the *casa* and stomped out on the log porch. There was a sick look of horror on his face. He mounted his horse and set spurs to it. The sound of the hoofs rattled on the hard gravel and died away on the river road beyond the great limestone house.

Lee led out a team hitched to a buggy. He led it to the front of the log house. He walked

240

back to get his horse, which Marsh had led back to the corral.

The woman came slowly to the door. She looked at the team and the buggy and then at the Kid. "You'll be needing a housekeeper," she said.

There was no answer from the Kid. She got into the buggy and picked up the reins. She touched up the team with a whip. She did not look back as she drove through the dark shadowed *bosque*.

Lee walked the dun to where the Kid was standing in the road looking toward the *bosque*. The Kid turned. "I'll need a good ramrod here now, Lee," he said. "How about it?"

Lee shook his head. "It's not my line of business. Goodbye, Kid."

The Kid watched him ride toward the *bosque*. "Where do I mail you the money?" he called out.

Lee turned in the saddle and rested a hand on the cantle. "Why," he said, "to General Delivery, Santa Fe."

"You planning on working up there?"

Lee shrugged. "I had an interesting proposition up there, Kid. I'm due for a little rest.

Thought I'd sort of scout out the lay of the land up there for future work."

"*Vaya con Dios*!" called out the Kid.

Lee did not look back. He raised his right hand and waggled it. In a little while, he was gone in the shadows, and the sound of the hoof beats was drowned out by the subdued roar of the Broken Bow.

THE END

FARGO: MASSACRE RIVER
by John Benteen

Fargo spurred his horse to the edge of the road. The ambushers up ahead had now blocked the road. Fargo's convoy was a jumble, a perfect target for the insurgents' weapons!

SUNDANCE:
DEATH IN THE LAVA
by John Benteen

The land echoed with the thundering hoofs of Modoc ponies. In minutes they swooped down and captured the wagon train and its cargo of gold. But now the halfbreed they called Sundance was going after it, and he swore nothing would stand in his way.

GUNS OF FURY
by Ernest Haycox

Dane Starr, alias Dan Smith, wanted to close the door on his past and hang up his guns, but people wouldn't let him. Good men wanted him to settle their scores for them. Bad men thought they were faster and itched to prove it. Starr had to keep killing just to stay alive.

FARGO: PANAMA GOLD
by John Benteen

Cleve Buckner was recruiting an army of killers, gunmen and deserters from all over Central America. With foreign money behind him, Buckner was going to destroy the Panama Canal before it could be completed. Fargo's job was to stop Buckner—and to eliminate him once and for all!

FARGO: THE SHARPSHOOTERS
by John Benteen

The Canfield clan, thirty strong, were raising hell in Texas. One of them had shot a Texas Ranger, and the Rangers had to bring in the killer. Fargo was tough enough to hold his own against the whole clan.

SUNDANCE: OVERKILL
by John Benteen

Sundance's reputation as a fighting man had spread. There was no job too tough for the halfbreed to handle. So when a wealthy banker's daughter was kidnapped by the Cheyenne, he offered Sundance $10,000 to rescue the girl.

HELL RIDERS
by Steve Mensing

Wade Walker's kid brother, Duane, was locked up in the Silver City jail facing a rope at dawn. Wade was a ruthless outlaw, but he was smart, and he had vowed to have his brother out of jail before morning!

DESERT OF THE DAMNED
by Nelson Nye

The law was after him for the murder of a marshal—a murder he didn't commit. Breen was after him for revenge—and Breen wouldn't stop at anything . . . blackmail, a frameup . . . or murder.

DAY OF THE COMANCHEROS
by Steven C. Lawrence

Their very name struck terror into men's hearts—the Comancheros, a savage army of cutthroats who swept across Texas, leaving behind a bloodstained trail of robbery and murder.

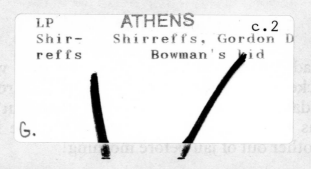

DESERT OF THE DAMNED

The law was after him for the murder of a marshal—a murder he didn't commit. Breen was after him for revenge—and Breen wouldn't stop at anything . . . blackmail, a frameup . . . or murder.

DAY OF THE COMANCHEROS
by Steven C. Lawrence

Their very name struck terror into men's hearts—the Comancheros, a savage army of cutthroats who swept across Texas, leaving behind a bloodstained trail of robbery and murder.

AC